SPECIAL REPORTS

DOMESTIC
TERRORISM

BY LAURA K. MURRAY

CONTENT CONSULTANT
ORLANDREW E. DANZELL, PHD
ASSOCIATE PROFESSOR, INTELLIGENCE ANALYSIS PROGRAM
JAMES MADISON UNIVERSITY

Essential Library

An Imprint of Abdo Publishing | abdobooks.com

abdobooks.com

Published by Abdo Publishing, a division of ABDO, PO Box 398166, Minneapolis, Minnesota 55439. Copyright © 2021 by Abdo Consulting Group, Inc. International copyrights reserved in all countries. No part of this book may be reproduced in any form without written permission from the publisher. Essential Library™ is a trademark and logo of Abdo Publishing.

Printed in the United States of America, North Mankato, Minnesota.
102020
012021

THIS BOOK CONTAINS
RECYCLED MATERIALS

Cover Photo: Richard Brian/Las Vegas Review-Journal/AP Images
Interior Photos: Liu Liwei/Xinhua/Chine Nouvelle/SIPA/Newscom, 4–5; Lola Gomez/ Austin American-Statesman/AP Images, 6; Cedar Attanasio/AP Images, 12; Red Line Editorial, 16–17; North Wind Picture Archives, 18–19; Everett Collection/Newscom, 25; Harold Valentine/AP Images, 28–29; Marty Lederhandler/AP Images, 33; AP Images, 37; Elaine Thompson/AP Images, 38–39; John Youngbear/AP Images, 40; NewsBase/ AP Images, 44; Jim Argo/The Daily Oklahoman/AP Images, 47; David Goldman/ AP Images, 50–51, 70–71; Jim Collins/AP Images, 52–53; Barry Chin/The Boston Globe/Getty Images, 57; Jack Plunkett/AP Images, 60–61; Stephen B. Morton/AP Images, 65; Matt Masin/The Orange County Register/AP Images, 68; Pablo Martinez Monsivais/AP Images, 73; Michael Nigro/Pacific Press/Sipa/AP Images, 77; Steve Helber/AP Images, 78–79; Alex Milan Tracy/Sipa USA/AP Images, 83, 88–89; Evan Vucci/AP Images, 86; Hyosub Shin/Atlanta Journal-Constitution/AP Images, 92; Mike Hardiman/Alamy, 98

Editor: Charly Haley
Series Designer: Maggie Villaume

Library of Congress Control Number: 2020940274

Publisher's Cataloging-in-Publication Data

Names: Murray, Laura K., author.
Title: Domestic terrorism / by Laura K. Murray
Description: Minneapolis, Minnesota : Abdo Publishing, 2021 | Series: Special reports
     | Includes online resources and index
Identifiers: ISBN 9781532194146 (lib. bdg.) | ISBN 9781098213503 (ebook)
Subjects: LCSH: Domestic terrorism--Juvenile literature. | Internal security--Juvenile
     literature. | National security--Juvenile literature. | Domestic terrorism--Law
     and legislation--Juvenile literature.
Classification: DDC 363.3251--dc23

CONTENTS

CHAPTER ONE

TERROR IN
EL PASO

It was a hot Saturday morning on August 3, 2019, in El Paso, Texas. Inside the huge Walmart Supercenter, up to 3,000 shoppers crowded the aisles, many browsing the back-to-school displays.[1] Others loaded their vehicles in the sprawling parking lot. Players, coaches, and parents from a girls' soccer team were stationed outside the store entrances selling snacks to help pay for new jerseys and tournament fees. As El Paso is located on the US–Mexico border across from Juárez, Mexico, many shoppers and employees were Hispanic.

Just before 10:40 a.m., 21-year-old Patrick Crusius opened fire in the parking lot. Armed with a semiautomatic rifle similar to an AK-47, he then entered

Texas state troopers, local police, and federal investigators all responded to the El Paso Walmart shooting.

the store and continued shooting. Store manager Robert Evans called out a "code brown" into his two-way radio, giving the alert for an active shooter.[2] Then he herded people out of the building as he shouted warnings to customers in English and Spanish. Another employee, Gilbert Serna, led dozens of customers and employees through a fire exit and hid them in shipping containers before ushering others to a nearby store. Some people hid under tables or between vending machines. Police and other emergency responders arrived on the scene at 10:45 a.m., six minutes after the first 911 call.[3] People used stock carts to wheel out the wounded for medical treatment.

People gathered for community vigils and memorial services to remember the victims of the El Paso shooting.

After the shooter, a white man from Texas, surrendered to authorities, he told them he had wanted to shoot as many Mexicans as he could. Soon after, authorities found a manifesto allegedly written by him online, posted just before the attack. The writings included anti-immigration sentiments and conspiracy theories supported by white nationalists that warned of a supposed "Hispanic invasion."[4] According to one person wounded in the attack, the shooter allowed non-Hispanic shoppers out of the building as the violence unfolded.

INFLAMMATORY LANGUAGE

Anti-immigrant phrases such as "Hispanic invasion" in the online manifesto linked to the El Paso gunman ignited debate over politicians' language. Critics alleged the manifesto reflected the language of President Donald Trump, whose campaign often referred to an "invasion" at the US–Mexico border. "People hate the word invasion, but that's what it is," Trump said in early 2019, referring to immigration. The El Paso gunman allegedly wrote that his views predated the president. A White House official called criticism that connected Trump's language and violence "unfortunate, unreasonable, and obviously politically motivated." Others noted that divisive language regarding an "invasion" of illegal immigrants had existed for decades before Trump's presidential campaign. But people still debated whether the president's words legitimized this idea for extremists.[5]

The shooting eventually left 23 people dead and more than 20 others injured. Of those killed, 14 were American citizens, eight were Mexican citizens, and one was

German.[6] The oldest killed was Luis Alfonso Juarez, age 90. The youngest was Javier Rodriguez, age 15. Rodriguez had been doing back-to-school shopping with his uncle, who was also shot but survived. The shooting was considered the deadliest anti-Hispanic attack in modern US history.

DEFINING DOMESTIC TERRORISM

The attack in El Paso came less than a week after a deadly shooting at a festival in Gilroy, California. Thirteen hours after the El Paso shooting, a gunman in Dayton, Ohio, shot 26 people within 32 seconds, nine of them fatally.[7] As communities mourned the onslaught of deadly shootings, holding candlelight vigils, donating blood, and making memorials for the victims, familiar debates exploded throughout the United States over gun laws, racism, and terrorism. Many citizens and political leaders called for the shooters, all born in the United States, to be labeled as terrorists, renewing conversations about what constitutes terrorism when perpetrated by Americans on US soil.

The federal government defines domestic terrorism as a criminal attack within the United States meant to intimidate or coerce civilians, influence government policy, or affect government conduct through mass destruction, political killings, or kidnapping. Federal laws also categorize more than 50 specific acts as crimes of terrorism, such as targeting an airport or using a weapon of mass destruction.

Although the US government defines domestic terrorism and has laws against many crimes that could be considered acts of domestic terrorism, it does not have a law that defines domestic terrorism itself as a federal crime. This means no one can be tried and punished in federal court on a criminal charge of domestic terrorism, though the person may be charged with similar crimes. More than 30 states have forms of anti-terrorism laws that make acts of terrorism crimes.[8] In the late 2010s and early 2020s, there was both widespread support and criticism for a new law that would make domestic terrorism a punishable federal crime.

MEXICO SUES

Following the attack in El Paso that killed eight of its citizens, Mexico announced that it would sue the United States for failing to protect Mexican people. "We consider this act an act of terrorism against the Mexican-American community and the Mexicans living in the United States," said Marcel Ebrard, Mexican foreign minister.[9] In 2019, the Mexican government helped relatives of people who had been killed sue Walmart for security failures. Mexican officials also sought to bring the shooter to Mexico to be charged with terrorism.

Supporters say a new law would provide federal agents with more resources for combating terrorism.

Alternately, voices across the political spectrum say this additional law isn't necessary and that existing laws adequately address domestic terrorism. Many concerns center on how an additional law would be enforced. For example, the American Civil Liberties Union (ACLU), a civil rights nonprofit organization, has said the enforcement of a new crime law would disproportionately target people of color and other marginalized communities. The group believes additional crime laws would contribute to the problem of communities of color being over-criminalized and punished.

Other critics say a new law would give the government too much power. They say the enforcement of such a law would infringe on free speech and lead to unjust punishments for people expressing their opinions. For example, they worry a political group could target the opposing side for protesting. They also say that someone could be targeted for comments that others view as racist or offensive, despite the fact that freedom of speech is protected under the First Amendment.

CHARGED WITH HATE

Following the El Paso attack, the federal government investigated the incident as a case of domestic terrorism. Because there was no existing federal law that would allow domestic terrorism to be prosecuted as a crime itself, the label of domestic terrorism was considered largely symbolic. Still, many people were glad to have the attack labeled this way.

"We are heartened that this has been recognized for what it is: a racially motivated terrorist attack on our safe and tranquil community," said Congresswoman Veronica Escobar of Texas. "The shooter came into our community because we are a Hispanic

WALMART GUN RESPONSE

Following the El Paso shooting, Walmart announced it would limit gun and ammunition sales. In a company memo, Walmart CEO Doug McMillon said the company would stop selling certain rifle ammunition and all handgun ammunition after selling off the ammunition in stock at the time. It would also stop selling handguns in Alaska. The store would continue to sell other types of guns and ammunition focused on hunting and sport shooting. In prior years, the store had stopped selling handguns and military-style rifles and raised the minimum purchase age for firearms. The memo asked that customers stop openly carrying guns in its stores in states that allowed the practice. The company also publicly asked the US Congress to act on gun reform. According to McMillon, these actions resulted from shootings in El Paso and elsewhere. "It's clear to us that the status quo is unacceptable," he said.[10]

community and because we have immigrants here. He
came here to harm us."[11]

In October 2019, the El Paso gunman pleaded not
guilty to capital murder charges brought by state court. In
February 2020, he was charged separately in federal court.
He faced 90 charges related to hate crimes and the use
of firearms.[12]

After the El Paso shooting, Representative Veronica Escobar, a Democrat
from Texas, was one of several politicians to speak out against gun
violence that stems from racism.

THE ENEMY AT HOME

Throughout the years, the US government's response to terrorism has evolved along with the changing world. Until 2001, the country had very few terrorism-related laws. One was the Security Assistance and Arms Export Control Act of 1976, which focused on international terrorism. September 11, 2001, now known as 9/11, marked a turning point. On that day, jihadist extremists hijacked four airplanes and crashed them into the World Trade Center in New York City, the Pentagon in Washington, DC, and a field in Pennsylvania. Nearly 3,000 people died in the attacks.

Following 9/11, the Federal Bureau of Investigation (FBI) and other federal agencies focused on disrupting terrorist plots before attacks could be carried out. In the following decades, conversations around terrorism centered on violent groups known as jihadist or Islamic extremists, which operate from foreign countries. These groups claim to engage in *jihad*, or holy war on

"WHITE SUPREMACY IS A GREATER THREAT THAN INTERNATIONAL TERRORISM RIGHT NOW. WE ARE BEING EATEN FROM WITHIN."[13]

—DAVID HICKTON, UNIVERSITY OF PITTSBURGH INSTITUTE FOR CYBER LAW, POLICY, AND SECURITY, 2019

behalf of the religion Islam. The most well-known of these terrorist organizations include the Islamic State of Iraq and Syria (ISIS) and al-Qaeda. Amid the conversations about terrorism from overseas, the El Paso shooting of 2019 was a stark reminder of a threat close to home.

Deadly acts of homegrown terrorism increased in the 2010s. From 2015 to 2018, the FBI arrested more suspects in investigations related to domestic terrorism than international terrorism. Deadly domestic attacks have been carried out by far-right extremists who hold white supremacist, anti-government, or antiabortion ideologies. There have also been attacks stemming from misogynistic and

THE EXTREMES

As in any group, extremists do not represent the beliefs of most. For instance, jihadist or Islamic extremists do not represent the beliefs of most Muslims. Right-wing extremists do not represent the beliefs of most conservatives, and left-wing extremists do not represent the beliefs of most liberals. Extremists are sometimes willing to commit violence for their beliefs. According to the FBI, violent extremists often exploit new recruits' fears and personal needs to make them believe violence is the only solution. "Violent extremists will tell you just about anything—including lies—to get you to support their cause," the FBI says on its website for teens. "Don't be a puppet. Just because someone sounds convincing or makes big promises doesn't mean you should join them in hurting innocent people."[14]

Black nationalist ideologies as well as animal rights or environmental extremism.

Discussions over domestic terrorism have often overlapped with topics such as racism, gun control, and abortion and reproductive rights. Counterterrorism investigators have harnessed the power of technology while battling new challenges brought by the internet and social media. In 2020, FBI director Christopher Wray called racially motivated violent extremism a threat equal to that of ISIS. Meanwhile, some critics have accused federal agencies of focusing disproportionately on international terrorists, particularly jihadist extremists, while not doing enough to tamp down violent white nationalist movements in the United States. The roots of today's domestic terrorism go all the way back to the beginning of the United States. Through the changing times, Americans have debated how to identify and combat the threats that are homegrown.

FROM THE
HEADLINES

STATE TERRORISM LAWS

While a federal domestic terrorism law does not exist, 34 states and Washington, DC, have some form of anti-terrorism laws.[15] These laws may generally define what terrorism is or specify prohibited activities. Twenty-seven of these states passed anti-terrorism laws in 2002 as a response to 9/11. Others have passed or changed laws in the wake of domestic terrorism incidents in their states. Many times, officials from both local and federal agencies will investigate a terrorism case. Other factors involved, such as where the crime took place or the means

These 34 states have some type of anti-terrorism law. The laws vary from state to state. States that do not have anti-terrorism laws still have other criminal laws to address incidents that could be considered domestic terrorism.

of attack the perpetrator used (such as a gun or bomb), can make determining criminal charges and pursuing a court case a complex process.

STATES WITH ANTI-TERRORISM LAWS

Alabama	Indiana	Missouri	South Dakota
Alaska	Iowa	Nevada	Tennessee
Arizona	Kansas	New Jersey	Utah
Arkansas	Kentucky	New York	Vermont
California	Louisiana	North Carolina	Virginia
Connecticut	Maine	Ohio	Washington
Florida	Massachusetts	Oklahoma	West Virginia
Georgia	Michigan	Pennsylvania	
Illinois	Minnesota	South Carolina	

CHAPTER TWO

EARLY FORMS
OF TERROR

A cts of violence and terror against various groups have happened at every stage of US history. As the nation has grown and changed, so have the tensions between people. These tensions have been tied closely to issues such as racism, nativism, and vigilantism. For instance, early European explorers and immigrants in North America terrorized and killed Native Americans in mass numbers, often drawing attacks in retaliation. Other groups targeted in the ensuing decades included religious groups, immigrants, labor leaders, and civil rights activists.

Groups experiencing persecution have also inflicted terror on others. In the mid-1600s, the Puritans famously

Some of the earliest acts of mass violence in what is now the United States included attacks back and forth between European colonists and Native Americans.

fled England for North America to escape religious persecution. However, the Puritans quickly turned on anyone who they viewed as an outsider. This was perhaps best demonstrated during the witch trials that took place in Salem, Massachusetts, in the late 1600s. Accusations of witchcraft resulted in widespread panic and unlawful trials. Nineteen innocent people were hanged, a man was pressed to death with stones, and others died in jail.

The idea of taking the law into one's own hands was prevalent in the 1700s and 1800s. Militias and vigilantism played large roles in the Revolutionary War (1775–1983) as the American colonies fought for independence from Great Britain.

In the 1800s, people on the western frontier banded together to carry out justice. An infamous case of militia violence occurred in September

VIGILANTISM

Vigilantism has long been a fixture in American consciousness, with historical figures and people in fictional stories taking it upon themselves to resist tyranny or protect their communities against outlaws. Famous fictional vigilantes include Robin Hood and Batman, who go against the system to deliver justice. But vigilantism has also spurred more problematic perspectives. According to historian Richard Maxwell Brown, it has been a way for people who see themselves as upright citizens to take part in activities such as lynching. In recent decades, it has contributed to the anti-government mindset of extremists advocating for the creation of militias and launching of military-style attacks.

1857 in southern Utah. A Mormon militia attacked an Arkansas wagon train traveling through the area on its way to California. Leading up to the incident, tensions were running high. The US government viewed the Mormons as rebels. The Mormons—who had fled to Utah some 30 years earlier after they experienced prejudice and violence from angry mobs in states such as New York, Ohio, and Missouri—experienced growing concern that the government would invade their settlements. They stockpiled food and weapons and became paranoid that outsiders would try to kill them. The Arkansas wagon train warded off the Mormons' attacks for several days. The Mormon militia eventually tricked them into leaving their wagon circle and brutally slaughtered 120 men, women, and children. The event became known as the Mountain Meadows Massacre.

TARGETING AFRICAN AMERICANS

The American Civil War (1861–1865), fought between the Northern states, or the Union, and the Southern states, or the Confederacy, marked a turning point in the nation's history and its relationship with terror. Although President

Abraham Lincoln's Emancipation Proclamation of 1863 declared that enslaved people in the Confederacy were legally free, the Southern states refused to recognize this. After the Union won the war in 1865, the United States was reunited as one country, and all slaves were freed under the law.

"ENSLAVED PEOPLE WERE PROMISED FREEDOM, AND WHAT THEY GOT WAS TERRORISM, AND IT WAS HORRIFIC."[1]

—BRYAN STEVENSON, FOUNDER OF EQUAL JUSTICE INITIATIVE, 2018

But many white Southerners believed African Americans should not have equal rights or protections. They wanted to keep control of politics, business, and other aspects of life. They were particularly concerned because African Americans outnumbered white people in some parts of the South. Mobs of white citizens proceeded to terrorize and kill African Americans for decades. White supremacist groups formed both in secret and openly. They used violence to oppress and intimidate African Americans and other people supporting them or voting for their interests.

Following the Civil War, incidents of lynching escalated. In these brutal acts of violence, mobs killed Black people without trials and often without any reason other than the person being Black. White people were not punished for these killings. Many people, including politicians, police, and other leaders, supported and took part in lynching. Southern white mobs killed an estimated 1,985 people between 1882 and 1903.[2] That number rose to an estimated 4,400 by 1950.[3] Violence against Black people, including lynching, riots, and other acts of terror, shaped the United States, as more than six million people fled the South during Reconstruction, the tumultuous period following the Civil War.

BOMBINGS OF THE EARLY 1900s

The United States changed in the late 1800s with the expansion of factories, manufacturing, and other labor as the country moved

KU KLUX KLAN

Considered one of the oldest and most notorious American hate groups, the Ku Klux Klan (KKK) formed in 1865 during Reconstruction. The group aimed to terrorize and take away the rights of African Americans and anyone who supported them. The KKK was present in nearly every Southern state by 1870. Known for their white hooded costumes, KKK members carried out violent attacks and murders. After a decline, the group revived in the 1920s with added emphasis on opposing immigration, Catholics, and Jews. The image of a fiery cross became a widely recognized symbol of hate after the group began burning crosses during its nighttime rituals. By 1925, the organization had an estimated four million members before declining again. Its next revival came in the 1960s during the civil rights movement as it attempted to uphold segregation policies through bombings and other killings. In 2019, the Southern Poverty Law Center (SPLC), a civil rights advocacy organization, estimated the KKK had between 5,000 and 8,000 members split between different organizations.[4]

away from farming during the time period known as the second Industrial Revolution. The US population—as well as its industrial workforce—tripled between 1860 and 1910.[5] A lack of worker rights and regulations led to dangerous and unfair working conditions, with children working in factories and women receiving less pay than men. People began to form labor unions to advocate for better working conditions. Labor extremists led rioting and carried out bombings in cities throughout the country.

In October 1910, a time bomb made of dynamite sticks and an alarm clock exploded outside the *Los Angeles Times* newspaper office in California. The bomb destroyed the building, killing 21 people and injuring dozens more.[6] It was the deadliest domestic terrorism attack on US soil up to that point. Two other bombs outside the homes of the newspaper's publisher and a businessman didn't detonate. The attackers were J. B. McNamara and his brother J. J. McNamara, the leader of an iron workers' labor union.

In November 1917, another infamous bombing occurred, this time at the Central Police Station in Milwaukee, Wisconsin. A 20-pound (9 kg) bomb was intended for a church, but it blew up at the police station after people brought in the suspicious package. It killed nine police officers and two civilians. No other event had killed more police officers in US history until the 9/11 terrorist attacks more than 80 years later. No one was ever arrested in relation to the bombing, but it was widely believed to have been perpetrated by a group of anarchists known as the Galleanists.

A similar bombing occurred on Wall Street in New York City in September 1920. A man stopped a horse-pulled cart on the busy street in front of the J. P. Morgan building, escaping before the bomb exploded and shot metal shards and flames into the air. One witness said, "I saw the explosion, a column of smoke shoot up into the air and then saw people dropping all around me, some of them

A crowd gathered to view the wreckage of the bombing at the *Los Angeles Times* office in 1910.

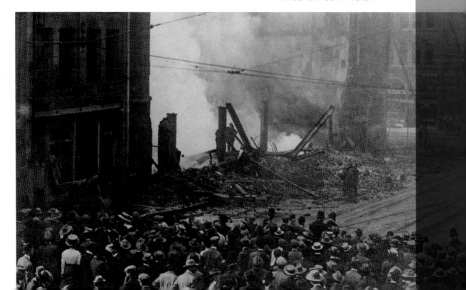

VIOLENCE AGAINST CHINESE IMMIGRANTS

The late 1800s saw a growth of movements against Asian immigrants. Throughout the 1850s, Chinese immigrants came to the western United States to work in the gold mines, on the railroads, and in other industries. As they found success and started their own businesses, resentment among other groups grew. Race-based attacks followed. In 1871, a mob massacred up to 20 Chinese residents in Los Angeles, California, in what was later described as a race riot.[9] Later legislation limited Chinese immigration. The Chinese Exclusion Act of 1882 stopped Chinese immigration to the United States and banned Chinese people from becoming US citizens. While the act was repealed in 1943, few Chinese immigrants were allowed annually until 1965, when Congress passed the Immigration and Nationality Act.

with their clothing afire."[7] The bombing killed 38 people and injured hundreds more. It would remain the deadliest terrorist attack on US soil until 1995. Wall Street reopened the next day, with crowds converging on the streets to sing "America the Beautiful."

People began to suspect anti-capitalist and anarchist groups, including possibly the Galleanists, were behind the Wall Street bombing. Postal workers uncovered flyers nearby that were signed the "American Anarchist Fighters."[8] Federal investigators worked on the case with help from the New York City police and fire departments, but the attackers were never identified. The FBI considers the Wall Street bombing one of its earliest terrorism cases.

MORE TO THE
STORY

TULSA RACE MASSACRE

In June 1921, Tulsa, Oklahoma, was the site of a deadly terror campaign against Black Americans. After a Black teenager rode in an elevator with a white woman, rumors and exaggerated stories spread through town. Convinced that Black Americans were staging an uprising, white mobs attacked Black people and looted and burned Black-owned businesses. At that time, much of Tulsa was segregated, with Black people and white people living apart. The mobs targeted the wealthy Black community of Greenwood District, known as Black Wall Street. Supported and armed by public officials, white citizens shot Black people in the streets and destroyed an estimated 1,200 homes, as well as churches, stores, a hospital, a library, and other buildings. The next morning, the riot ended with the arrival of the National Guard, which imprisoned nearly all of the area's Black residents. Although the official reported death count was 36, historians estimate that up to 300 people were killed, while hundreds were injured and thousands of Black people were left homeless. Authorities covered up the incident for decades. In 1996, Oklahoma lawmakers authorized a commission to review the event. In 2001, the commission released its final report, stating, "Despite duties to preserve order and to protect property, no government at any level offered adequate resistance, if any at all, to what amounted to the destruction of the Greenwood neighborhood."[10]

CHAPTER THREE

THE 1960s
AND 1970s

The 1960s and 1970s brought a new age of terrorism both in the United States and globally. During this time, modern-day terrorism developed with the formation of extremist groups intent on terrorizing others to further their own beliefs and agendas. In the United States, hundreds of attacks occurred annually by the 1970s, including bombings, shootings, and airplane hijackings. The turbulent political and social change during this era played a role in many of the terrorists' motivations.

Renewed violence based in racism continued in the South alongside the developing civil rights movement in which Black Americans worked to gain equal rights. White supremacy groups resurged throughout the

As violence based in racism continued into the 1960s, Black Americans and others worked to protest against it.

1960s, carrying out murders and bombings while holding rallies and marches to speak out against Black Americans, Catholics, Jews, and labor unions. On September 15, 1963, members of the United Klans of America, part of the Ku Klux Klan (KKK), detonated a bomb at a Black Baptist church in Birmingham, Alabama, killing four girls between the ages of 11 and 14.

RISE OF THE EXTREME LEFT

Meanwhile, extremist groups with leftist views began to form in the late 1960s, determined to create revolution through violence. Throughout the 1960s and 1970s, several extremist groups had anti-war, anti-capitalist, or anti-authority beliefs, motivated by communism and other liberal ideals. Some groups, often made up of college students, carried out protest bombings. Violence also came from some cultural and nationalist groups, such as the Black Liberation Army (BLA), who wanted to end the oppression of Black Americans, and Puerto Rico separatists, who sought Puerto Rican independence from the United States. By the mid-1970s, terrorist activity in the United States had shifted into a much more violent phase.

Domestic terrorists used several strategies during this time, including assassinations, bombings, kidnappings, and armed assaults. Many of these tactics had been used for centuries, but extremists made them a regular occurrence throughout the 1970s. Between 1971 and 1972, an estimated 2,500 bombings occurred in the United States. *Time* magazine recounted a New York City woman telling a reporter in 1977, "Oh, another bombing? Who is it this time?"[1] Adding to the difficulty, the modern concept of terrorism was just emerging. Government and law enforcement officials had to figure out how to combat the attacks. CNN retrospectively labeled the 1970s as the "golden age of terrorism."[2]

FOR PUERTO RICO

Throughout the 1970s and 1980s, some domestic terrorists carried out attacks with the goal of separating Puerto Rico from the United States. They wanted Puerto Rico, a US territory, to be free of the United States' economic and political control. Two prominent groups in this effort were Fuerzas Armadas de Liberación Nacional (FALN) and Los Macheteros. FALN formed in the mainland United States, with its members carrying out dozens of bombings in places such as New York City and Chicago, Illinois, while other groups formed and mainly carried out attacks in Puerto Rico. FALN in particular was professionally organized as a military-type operation. Its attacks were mainly bombings targeting office and government buildings, banks, and other establishments. Its goals were to damage the government authority and gain support for its cause. The group's deadliest attack was in January 1975, when a bomb in New York City killed four people and injured more than 50.[3]

BLACK LIBERATION ARMY

Operating from 1970 to 1981, the BLA was a Black militant group focused on fighting against the US government and liberating Black Americans from oppression. The BLA was mostly made up of people who had left the Black Panther Party, a civil rights group. The BLA carried out bombings, murders, robberies, and prison breaks. In 1977, noted BLA figure Assata Shakur was sentenced to life in prison for killing a police officer during a traffic stop. BLA members helped her escape prison in 1979. In 2013, the FBI put Shakur, godmother to rap legend Tupac Shakur, on its top-ten list of most-wanted terrorists. Her defenders held up her innocence and accused the authorities of unfairly targeting her. In 2020, Shakur was still on the run.

WEATHER UNDERGROUND

In March 1970, a bomb accidentally exploded in the basement of a New York City townhome. It took investigators days to dig through the rubble looking for body parts and clues. They established that three people who had been making the bomb had been killed. All were members of a radical group called the Weather Underground. Two others had fled. Police found dynamite, bombs, and other bomb-making equipment at the scene.

The Weather Underground formed in 1969. It had about 100 members, mostly college students, across the country. Sometimes called the Weatherman or Weathermen, the group took its name from Bob Dylan lyrics and was a branch of another group, Students

A New York City townhome burns in 1970 as a result of explosions caused by members of the Weather Underground making bombs.

for a Democratic Society. The Weather Underground opposed racism, corporate greed, and the United States' involvement in the Vietnam War (1954–1975). The group called for war against the US government, writing in its 1974 manifesto, "Our intention is to disrupt the empire . . . to incapacitate it, to put pressure on the cracks."[4] Throughout the 1970s, the group set off more than two dozen bombs at government and public buildings, including the US Capitol, the Pentagon, the State Department, and police stations.

The FBI labeled the Weather Underground a terrorist organization and spent several years trying to capture its members. The inclusion of the Weather Underground on the FBI's Most Wanted List served to make the group famous across the country. The group was eventually brought down in large part due to New York's Anti-Terrorist Task Force formed by the FBI and New York City police. Between 1977 and 1980, the Weather Underground's activities fizzled out as most members blended back into society, as did many other radicals of the era.

THE WOMEN OF M19

As activities of some groups de-escalated, other far-left groups were ramping up, including an all-woman group founded in 1978. These women called their group the May 19th Communist Organization (M19), a reference to the birthday of two of their heroes: Vietnamese leader Ho Chi Minh and American civil rights leader Malcolm X. Some of the members had also been part of the Weather Underground. According to national security expert and historian William Rosenau, in the United States, the organization was "the first and only women-created and women-led terrorist group."[5]

Focused on political revolution, M19's activities soon turned extreme as they robbed armored trucks and detonated bombs at government buildings. No one was killed in these attacks. M19 also helped other extremists escape from prison, including leaders of the BLA and the Puerto Rican separatist group Fuerzas Armadas de Liberación Nacional. Often M19's activities were to show support for revolutions happening around the world or to protest the United States' role in what they saw as global injustices. Members were eventually arrested or became fugitives.

KIDNAPPING AN HEIRESS

Another leftist terror organization, the Symbionese Liberation Army (SLA), was active between 1973 and 1975. Inspired by radicalism

JEWISH DEFENSE LEAGUE

Designated as a right-wing terrorist group by the FBI and as a hate group by the SPLC, the Jewish Defense League (JDL) formed in 1968 in New York City. The JDL began as a vigilante-type group to protect Jewish people from anti-Semitic riots and attacks. Although the JDL claimed to defend Jewish people, its own mission was considered racist and extremist. Throughout the 1970s and 1980s, the JDL carried out bombings, assassinations, burglaries, and other attacks.

The JDL did target neo-Nazis, a hate group whose beliefs are inspired by Adolf Hitler's German Nazi Party, which violently attempted to exterminate Jewish people in the 1930s and 1940s. However, the JDL also targeted Soviets, Muslims, and foreign diplomats, as well as Jewish leaders who did not support its extremist views. Other American Jewish organizations denounced the JDL's activities. The JDL's leader was assassinated in 1990 by an Islamic extremist. The JDL was considered inactive in the United States in 2020, but it had active followers online and had chapters in other countries.

that called for war against the US government, the SLA carried out bank robberies, murders, and other crimes. The group became known for its February 1974 kidnapping of 19-year-old Patricia Hearst in Berkeley, California. As Hearst was an heiress, the granddaughter of famous newspaperman Randolph Hearst, her kidnapping captivated national interest—just as the SLA intended.

The FBI searched for Hearst. But the investigation took an unexpected turn when audiotapes revealed Hearst had joined the SLA and had taken a new name. In April 1974, Hearst appeared on security camera footage during a bank robbery in San Francisco, California. The video showed her holding a machine gun and yelling at bank customers. In another incident, Hearst was seen shooting the outside of a store.

RAID ON SLA HIDEOUT

In May 1974, authorities heard that the SLA was hiding out in a house in Los Angeles. Five hundred members of the Los Angeles Police Department surrounded the house. They fired approximately 1,200 rounds of ammunition into the house and threw in tear gas, which started a fire.[7] The SLA did not surrender. All six members inside were killed.

The FBI finally captured Hearst in September 1975. Although Hearst reported being brainwashed, drugged, assaulted, and forced to take part in the SLA's activities,

Patricia Hearst, *right*, is led to court in handcuffs for her trial in 1976. Jurors listened to more than 200 hours of testimony before finding Hearst guilty.

she was sentenced to seven years in prison for her role

in the bank robbery. President Jimmy Carter lessened

her sentence after two years, and president Bill Clinton

pardoned her in 2001. The FBI later called the kidnapping

"one of the strangest cases in FBI history."[8] By 1975, the

SLA had disbanded with its members killed, captured, or

on the run. Soon, the FBI would have its hands full with

another case of domestic terrorism that kept the public in

fear for 17 years—this time, the work of a single person.

CHAPTER FOUR

EMERGENCE OF THE LONE ATTACKER

In December 1993, computer science professor David Gelernter opened a package that had been sent to his office at Yale University. It exploded, leaving Gelernter with severe burns, shrapnel wounds, fractures, and damage to one eye. He also lost several fingers. The attack was the latest in a string of mail bombings against random victims that had begun in May 1978 by an unknown attacker nicknamed the Unabomber. The name came from the bomber's targets, which had been universities and airlines.

For nearly 20 years, the Unabomber led the FBI on one of its longest and most expensive manhunts in

After their yearslong search, FBI agents finally found the Unabomber's hideout in Montana.

history. He carried out attacks with homemade bombs that left no traceable evidence, all while taunting and threatening the public. The attacks, which lasted until 1995, sparked widespread fear and eventually left three people dead and 23 injured.[1]

The FBI finally zeroed in on the suspect, arresting him in a remote Montana cabin in April 1996. Ted Kaczynski had been a gifted student and assistant professor of mathematics. However, he left his teaching career in 1969 and soon decided to wage a violent campaign against modern technology. Fifty-three years old at the time of

As part of the security measures for Kaczynski's trial, federal agents escort him to court in handcuffs.

his arrest, he was punished with eight life sentences for the attacks, putting him in prison for the rest of his life. Though he was not charged as a terrorist, the case became one of the nation's most notorious examples of domestic terrorism.

The Unabomber represented a new kind of domestic terrorist drawing public attention: the so-called lone wolf. This controversial label referred to a person, nearly always a man, who acted alone or with little help to carry out violent attacks against the public. Kaczynski wasn't the first attacker to fit this description, but he would be cited often in discussions about this type of domestic terrorist.

LONE WOLF

Lone wolf attacks gained new notoriety in the 2010s as domestic terror attacks committed by individuals increased. Authorities scrambled to track motivations, profiles, and tendencies of the various individuals carrying out the attacks, in part to determine how to prevent more attacks from happening. The Department of Justice has since established two databases of these attacks for analysis. The term *lone wolf* has been criticized as being disproportionately applied to white attackers, while other attackers, such as jihadist extremists, are more quickly labeled terrorists.

LEGACIES OF RUBY RIDGE AND WACO

By the 1990s, right-wing extremism had overtaken the left-wing extremism of previous decades as the most dangerous domestic terrorism threat, according

to Dale L. Watson of the FBI's Counterterrorism and

Counterintelligence Division. Right-wing hate groups

and militias that emerged, such as the white supremacist

groups Aryan Nations and The Order, both out of the

Pacific Northwest, were mainly motivated by racist

and anti-government beliefs. Other domestic terrorists were focused on antiabortion agendas.

Major incidents in Idaho and Texas in the early 1990s affected many Americans' trust in government and inflamed the rage of right-wing extremists and domestic terrorists. In 1992, federal agents engaged in an 11-day standoff with the Randy and Vicki Weaver family at their property in Ruby Ridge, Idaho. The Weavers were anti-government religious fundamentalists who had been hoarding illegal weapons and had alleged ties to the Aryan Nations white

FALL OF COMMUNISM

By the 1980s, many of the left-wing domestic terrorism groups of the previous decades had been disbanded. This was due in a large part to the fall of communist regimes in Eastern Europe that culminated with the collapse of the Soviet Union in 1991. Many of the leftist terrorist groups had based their beliefs in communism and had also received funding from the Soviet Union throughout the 1960s and 1970s. Without the ideals and funding of communism, the groups disappeared.

supremacist group. Randy Weaver had sold illegal guns to an undercover agent from the federal Bureau of Alcohol, Tobacco, Firearms, and Explosives (ATF).

Authorities and the Weavers fired gunshots at each other during the second day of the standoff. Three people—Vicki Weaver, the Weavers' teenage son Samuel, and a US marshal—were killed in the exchange. Randy Weaver, his other children, and their family friend surrendered more than a week later. The Ruby Ridge siege was controversial, with many Americans viewing it as a tragedy after reviews of the case cited issues with how federal authorities handled it. People particularly criticized the killing of Vicki Weaver, who was holding her infant daughter when she was shot by an FBI sharpshooter.

The following year, ATF agents raided a compound near Waco, Texas. The compound was home to an extreme religious group called the Branch Davidians. The agents tried to arrest the group's leader, who claimed to be a prophet, on weapons charges. After a shoot-out, four agents and six Branch Davidians were dead, resulting in a 51-day standoff that gripped the nation's attention. When the remaining members refused to surrender, nearly

Federal agents search through the ruins of the Branch Davidians' compound in Waco after the fires that killed dozens of people inside.

900 federal agents and tactical team members surrounded the compound as the group barricaded itself inside with stockpiles of weapons, food, water, and gas masks.[2]

On April 19, 1993, the FBI launched tear gas into the compound, reportedly because of child abuse occurring inside. Soon after, fires broke out and more than 75 men, women, and children inside the compound died.[3] Some were found to have died by gunshot wounds. Critics have continued to debate whether the federal agents or the Branch Davidians were responsible for the fire and whether members of the Branch Davidians inflicted the gunshot wounds on themselves. A congressional investigation in 2000 concluded that government agents did not start the fires or shoot into the compound.

Feelings of anger, resentment, and disillusionment toward the government would reverberate for decades through the consciousness of many who were critical of the events at Ruby Ridge and Waco. Many of these critics cited the incidents as proof of government conspiracy and overreach. Ruby Ridge and Waco partially inspired lone attackers and also helped spur the growth of homegrown militias in the United States, poised to carry out extremist beliefs through violence. Militias eventually cropped up in all 50 states, often recruiting members at gun shows or public meetings. Throughout the 1990s, militia groups carried out or plotted various bombings on places such as government buildings, gay bars, and abortion clinics.

"I THINK OF [RUBY RIDGE] AS THE PRECURSOR FOR THE LAST COUPLE, [OR] THREE DECADES OF EXTREMISM BECAUSE IT COMBINED TWO THINGS: WHITE SUPREMACY AND RAGE AGAINST THE GOVERNMENT, AND THAT IS EXACTLY THE SAME TWO MOVEMENTS ON THE FAR RIGHT THAT HAS ANIMATED EXTREMISM ON THE FAR RIGHT UP UNTIL TODAY."[4]

—HEIDI BEIRICH, INTELLIGENCE PROJECT OF SOUTHERN POVERTY LAW CENTER, 2017

RISE OF THE MILITIA

With the events at Ruby Ridge and Waco spurring outrage at the federal government, the early 1990s saw the rise of homegrown militias in what became known as the Patriot movement. The groups focused on arming themselves, refusing to pay taxes, and not answering to the government. Timothy McVeigh, who committed the 1995 Oklahoma City bombing, was deeply invested in the ideas and conspiracy theories associated with the militia movement. By the end of the decade, the movement had declined, but it would be revitalized by the 2010s. According to the SPLC, the renewed militia wave was more racially motivated than the past movement.

OKLAHOMA CITY BOMBING

At 9:02 a.m. on April 19, 1995, a bomb inside a parked rental truck exploded outside the nine-story Alfred P. Murrah Federal Building in downtown Oklahoma City, Oklahoma. The bombing killed 168 people and injured hundreds more.[5] Nineteen children were killed, as the building had a day care on its second floor. The building had also been the site of local offices for the Social Security Administration, the Secret Service, the Department of Veterans Affairs, the Drug Enforcement Administration, ATF, and the US military. Much of the building collapsed, and hundreds of other buildings were damaged or destroyed. It is the deadliest domestic terrorism attack in US history.

Many people immediately assumed the attack was the work of foreign terrorists, as had been the case with

A crowd of people gathers at the site of the Oklahoma City bombing for a memorial to honor the victims.

similar bombings two years earlier at the World Trade Center parking garage in New York City. However, the FBI quickly discovered the attacker was a homegrown terrorist named Timothy McVeigh. He was a former US Army soldier with extreme right-wing, anti-government, and anti–law enforcement beliefs. McVeigh had been deeply angered by the government's actions during the Waco standoff. He carried out the Oklahoma City bombing on the two-year anniversary of the deaths in Waco.

McVeigh was convicted on federal murder charges in 1997 and received the death penalty. He later said he had no sympathy for people affected by the bombing and referred to the victims as "collateral damage."[6] In 2001, McVeigh was executed by lethal injection. The building that McVeigh bombed was later demolished, and a park with a memorial was built in its place. The nation had watched the footage of the Oklahoma City carnage in disbelief. But soon a different type of catastrophic terrorist attack would change the world forever.

MORE TO THE STORY

THE ORDER

Between 1983 and 1984, The Order leapt into headlines for its terrorist activities. Focused on eliminating Jewish and nonwhite people as well as revolting against the government, the group created a hit list of enemies. It attacked a synagogue in Boise, Idaho, and soon after fatally shot well-known Jewish radio host Alan Berg outside his home in Colorado. The group was also guilty of robberies, counterfeiting, and other crimes. One of the leaders was killed in a shoot-out with the FBI in 1984. Other members were arrested and charged with various sentences.

The Order took its name and strategy from a 1978 novel called *The Turner Diaries*, which was written by a neo-Nazi leader. The book became a key piece of propaganda for white nationalists and would continue to inspire right-wing extremists for decades, including the Oklahoma City bomber Timothy McVeigh in 1995 and members of the alt-right movement in the 2010s. The book's plot centered on a future world in which nonwhite people have oppressed white Americans and have taken their guns. In the book, white nationalists stage a violent uprising, killing nonwhite people and those who associate with them. Members of The Order referred to the book as their bible as they plotted their activities. "They were following *Turner Diaries* like a map," retired FBI agent Tom McDaniel said.[7]

FROM THE
HEADLINES

CATCHING THE UNABOMBER

The Unabomber's efforts to leave no trace included avoiding fingerprints, removing identifying marks from batteries, and making his own glue. Occasionally, the Unabomber sent letters to the media and his victims, and FBI profilers analyzed the writer's use of language and writing style to estimate his age and probable origins. But authorities still didn't have a solid lead.

In September 1995, a break in the case appeared. The Unabomber sent a manifesto to media outlets, saying that if a major newspaper printed the entire 35,000-word document, he would "desist from terrorism."[8] Titled "Industrial Society and Its Future,"

Letters sent by the Unabomber and writings provided by Ted Kaczynski's brother were crucial in federal agents' identification and arrest of Kaczynski.

the manifesto railed against the supposed evil of technology and science, along with other aspects of modern life.

Authorities debated whether to print the document, thereby giving a terrorist's views a wide audience. Hoping the letter would generate a reader tip, government officials eventually told newspapers to publish it. The letter was printed in the *Washington Post* and the *New York Times*, sparking many tips, including one from David Kaczynski, who came forward with information about his brother, Ted. David also provided letters and writings of Ted's. FBI criminal profiler James R. Fitzgerald remembered analyzing one of the documents and noting incredible similarities to the manifesto. He told his boss that either someone was playing an elaborate prank or "you've got your man."[9] The FBI used the linguistic analysis along with other evidence and new information about Ted Kaczynski's life to finally capture the Unabomber.

CHAPTER FIVE

A TURNING
POINT

The effects of the devastating September 11, 2001, terrorist attack on the United States rippled through all aspects of American life and security. The attack affected the future of US law enforcement, air travel, immigration, and cybersecurity. Over the next decade, news and fears of international terrorism dominated the headlines. However, the majority of terrorist attacks in the United States each year continued to be committed by domestic terrorists, including in 2001.

Following the 9/11 attacks, the US government underwent major restructuring to strengthen security and counterterrorism. Agencies created after 9/11 included the Department of Homeland Security (DHS),

Although the September 11 attacks were committed by foreign terrorists, they renewed some conversations about domestic terrorism as well.

which brought together nearly two dozen agencies under one department with the mission of protecting the country. Laws such as the 2001 USA PATRIOT Act expanded the powers of government departments and law enforcement in fighting terrorism, but critics said these powers were examples of government overreach.

THE USA PATRIOT ACT

In 2001, Congress passed the USA PATRIOT Act, which stood for Uniting and Strengthening America by Providing Appropriate Tools Required to Intercept and Obstruct Terrorism. It was signed into law by President George W. Bush. Some politicians supported the law as a way to protect the country against terrorists and expand the tools of counterterrorism investigators. Critics, however, denounced the broad powers it provided to government agencies without checks and balances. The law controversially expanded the government's ability to conduct surveillance, which critics saw as making it easy for the government to spy on its own citizens. The act also gave permission for the FBI to conduct searches without court orders and allowed immigrants to be detained indefinitely without trial.

Other laws looked to create more efficient ways to analyze and respond to intelligence information. In 2004, Congress passed the Intelligence Reform and Terrorism Prevention Act, which created the position of Director of National Intelligence (DNI) as well as the National Counterterrorism Center. The DNI oversees US intelligence agencies and advises the president. The National Counterterrorism Center's role eventually included keeping databases, analyzing data, and strategizing against international and domestic terrorism.

For the FBI's part, its Counterterrorism Division, established in 1999, saw its funding and operations increase after 9/11. The agency also had a new focus. "The FBI's new, more focused mission is the prevention of future terrorist attacks," announced J. T. Caruso of the Counterterrorism and Counterintelligence Division in 2002.[1] For many people, 9/11 had opened their eyes to dangers that had once seemed unthinkable.

> "TODAY, AMERICAN FEARS ARE DRIVEN NOT BY WHAT DAMAGE TERRORISTS HAVE DONE IN THE UNITED STATES SINCE 9/11, BUT BY THE FEAR THAT TOMORROW'S TERRORISTS WILL CARRY OUT ATTACKS OF EVEN GREATER SCALE."[3]
>
> —JOURNALIST BRIAN MICHAEL JENKINS, 2015

BIOLOGICAL TERRORISM

Shortly after the 9/11 terror attacks, people around the United States began receiving letters through the mail that were laced with anthrax spores, bacteria that caused the infectious disease of anthrax. Five people were killed and another 17 fell ill.[2] These letters were a biological terrorist attack. This type of attack uses germs to sicken or kill people, livestock, or crops. It was not the first time that anthrax had been used as a weapon, but this case represented the deadliest biological attack in the country's history.

The ensuing investigation, which investigators called Amerithrax, lasted for years as the FBI and other investigators pursued leads. In 2008, authorities announced that they would be bringing charges against Dr. Bruce Ivins, a biodefense researcher at the US Army Medical Research Institute of Infectious Diseases. The Maryland institute was the main research facility tasked with researching how to counter biological warfare. Before the charges were filed, Ivins killed himself. A 2011 report concluded that the scientific evidence pointed to Ivins but did not prove for certain that he was responsible. Although Ivins was suspected, the case

CYBER WARNINGS

In the early 2000s, authorities warned of the terrorism dangers posed by technology and the internet. The USA PATRIOT Act of 2001 modified the federal definition of terrorism to include computer activities. The FBI cautioned that cyberterrorists could use technology to shut down important energy or transportation infrastructure to cripple the country. In the decades since, social media has emerged as a way for both international and domestic terrorists to share radical beliefs and inspire others to take up their cause.

has not been officially classified as an act of domestic or international terrorism.

The threat of biological weapons was used by another domestic terrorist in 2001. Clayton Waagner, an antiabortion extremist, mailed more than 500 letters to abortion providers. The mailed envelopes included white powder that the letters claimed was anthrax, although it was not. Waagner professed to be a member of the Army

Amid the Amerithrax attacks, many places, including political and media offices, carefully screened their mail as a precaution against anthrax.

of God, a loosely organized terrorist group focused on killing abortion providers.

ECOTERRORISM

In the early 2000s, government officials warned of the threat posed by extremists focused on animal rights and environmental rights. Their activities were collectively referred to as ecoterrorism. Two of the most active groups were the Animal Liberation Front (ALF) and the Earth Liberation Front (ELF). In 2005, federal authorities announced they had opened 58 investigations into attacks by the two groups since 1999, mostly involving arson.[4]

Most ecoterrorism attacks were directed at property rather than people. ELF's attacks included setting fires or damaging property at vehicle dealerships and construction sites. In 2002, ELF set fire to construction equipment in Pennsylvania that was being used to clear trees. The same year, ELF and ALF claimed joint responsibility for releasing 250 minks from a Pennsylvania fur farm and later burning down a barn at the site. In 2003, ELF started fires in San Diego, California, at the site of a large condo complex, causing an estimated $20 million in damages.[6] Meanwhile, members of ALF claimed responsibility for setting fires and carrying out bombings at research labs as well as pharmaceutical and cosmetic facilities that performed animal testing.

THE GREEN SCARE

In the early 2000s, many activists criticized the government's treatment and sentencing of environmental and animal rights activists. They believed activists from organizations such as ALF and ELF were unfairly labeled as terrorists and saddled with disproportionate punishments for crimes that didn't harm humans. They called the government actions the "Green Scare," a reference to the Red Scare of the 1950s and 1960s when the government prosecuted suspected communists.[7] Others questioned the federal government's focus on ecoterrorism over more violent threats such as white supremacy. However, others held that the animal and environmental extremists deserved to be called terrorists for their harmful acts of arson and vandalism.

CHAPTER SIX

EXTREMISM
TAKES HOLD

O n November 5, 2009, US Army soldier Megan Martinez thought the gunshots ringing out on the military base in Fort Hood, Texas, were part of a training exercise. But the shots were coming from Major Nidal Hasan, an army psychiatrist who was rampaging through the base armed with a semiautomatic pistol. He was yelling, "Allahu Akbar," an Arabic phrase that translates to "God is great" in English.[1] When the soldier next to Martinez was shot, Martinez ducked down to the floor. Hasan continued shooting. "He was firing at anyone moving," Sergeant Maria Guerra later testified. "I see bodies, bodies everywhere."[2] By the time the gunman was nonfatally

An army sergeant comforts his wife at the scene of the Fort Hood mass shooting.

shot by security officers, 13 people were dead and more than 30 were wounded.[3]

Hasan, a 32-year-old Muslim man from Virginia, had become radicalized over the internet. Investigations after the shooting found that his coworkers had reported concerns about his extreme beliefs. He had been scheduled to deploy to Afghanistan soon after the shooting and reportedly wanted to stop Americans from going there and killing Muslims. He was paralyzed from the chest down after being shot by security officers during his attack at Fort Hood.

"TERRORISM IS NOT AN EXCEPTION, A ONE-OFF, A RANDOM THING. IT IS DEEPLY INGRAINED IN OUR POLITICS AND SOCIETY AND HISTORY."[4]

—WILLIAM ROSENAU, NATIONAL SECURITY EXPERT AND HISTORIAN

The case again brought up the complicated subject of what types of violent attacks should be labeled *terrorism*. This subject would continue to be debated as high-profile domestic terrorism attacks continued throughout the 2010s. Victims of the Fort Hood shooting called for the case to be labeled as terrorism. Organizations such as the National Counterterrorism Center and US State Department counted the incident as a terrorist attack.

Hasan faced a court-martial, where he was charged with 13 counts of premeditated murder and 32 counts of attempted murder. During the trial, Hasan admitted to being the shooter and pledged allegiance to the mujahideen, jihadist fighters. He served as his own attorney but made no attempt to defend himself. After being found guilty on all counts, he was sentenced to death.

TERROR IN HOLY PLACES

In 2012, another mass shooting occurred, this time in Oak Creek, Wisconsin. The shooter, 40-year-old Wade Michael Page, attacked a Sikh temple, killing seven people and wounding four others. He died of a self-inflicted gunshot wound after being shot by police. Page

WHITE SUPREMACY ON MILITARY BASES

The Oak Creek shooter's military history sparked ongoing discussions around extremism in the military. The shooter had reported his extremist views intensified during his time stationed at Fort Bragg military base in North Carolina in the 1990s, where white supremacists were open about their views. The base had made headlines around that time when, in December 1995, two neo-Nazi members of the US Army's 82nd Airborne Division randomly murdered a Black couple. Further investigations found that other soldiers on the base had white supremacist links. The case resulted in a sweeping investigation of extremism in the US military, as well as congressional hearings. The army began training against extremism and regulating extremist activities, but people continued to question whether enough was being done to stem recruitment by extremist groups near military bases.

was a white supremacist army veteran who had been born in Colorado. The investigating Joint Terrorism Task Force, one of the FBI's approximately 200 local terrorism defense groups, called the event a domestic terrorism incident.

According to the SPLC, the Oak Creek attack was part of a wave of domestic terrorist attacks that began in response to the 2008 election of Barack Obama as the first Black president of the United States. The SPLC asserted that the violent attacks by white supremacists and others intensified at their perceived loss of white power. It was the latest in a grouping of attacks against Sikh Americans since 9/11, as they had become targets for people who wrongfully associated them with jihadist extremists. The Oak Creek attack led to a congressional hearing on hate crimes. "It should cause all of us to redouble our efforts to combat the threat of domestic terrorism," said Senator Dick Durbin of Illinois.[5] The gunman had long been a follower of white supremacy.

Another attack on a place of worship occurred when a white supremacist shot and killed nine people at a historically Black church in Charleston, South Carolina, on June 17, 2015. The shooter, a 21-year-old white man named Dylann Roof, attended a prayer meeting at Mother Emanuel African Methodist Episcopal Church before opening fire on the group inside. He shot nine people, killing all of them. The shooter made racist statements during the attack and confessed soon after. Authorities quickly discovered his racist manifestos online and photos of him posing with the Confederate flag and other white supremacist symbols. He later said he carried out the attack because he wanted to kill Black people and had no remorse.

People gathered outside Mother Emanuel church to pray for the shooting victims.

Following the shooting, hundreds of demonstrators marched in the streets of Charleston, chanting, "Black lives matter." Artists created murals to memorialize the victims. "What Roof didn't understand when he walked into that church was the genius of Black America's survival and the nature of our overcoming," Rachel Kaadzi Ghansah, a Black essayist, wrote in 2017.[6] Roof was convicted of federal murder charges and hate crimes in 2017 and was sentenced to death. His attorneys appealed the sentence in 2020, claiming that he had not been competent to represent himself at his original trial. In the years following the murders, Roof continued to gain notoriety among white supremacist groups who saw him as a hero to emulate.

CONFEDERATE MONUMENTS

The racially motivated Charleston church shooting resulted in renewed scrutiny of Confederate statues and memorials on public sites throughout the United States. Most of the nation's Confederate monuments were built from the late 1890s to the 1960s. The debate continued for the next several years, leading to the removal of several Confederate statues. Supporters of these removals said the monuments had championed the racism of the past. Meanwhile, critics characterized the removals as erasing history.

ATTACK IN SAN BERNARDINO

The same year as the Charleston shooting, a husband and wife killed 14 people and wounded 24 others in San Bernardino, California.[7] Syed Farook and Tashfeen Malik attacked county public health employees at the regional treatment center where Farook worked on December 2, 2015. A large group had gathered for training and a holiday party when the two attackers entered with semiautomatic rifles. After a vehicle chase, law enforcement killed both in a shoot-out.

The San Bernardino killers were examples of extremists who had been radicalized over the internet. Farook had been born in the United States, while Malik was an immigrant from Pakistan. The couple had become followers of violent, radical jihadism online and soon made plans to carry out attacks against innocent people. They had stockpiled weapons and bomb-making supplies at their home before the attack.

EXTREME ISLAM AND TERROR ATTACKS

Following the San Bernardino attacks, discussions resurfaced regarding the role of Islam in terrorism.

Islamic leaders condemned the attacks and denounced extremist beliefs that encouraged violence. The Council on American-Islamic Relations (CAIR) reported an increase in anti-Muslim attacks after the San Bernardino shooting, including vandalism, threats, and assault. In Philadelphia, Pennsylvania, a person threw a severed pig's head at a mosque. In Florida, a man broke the windows of the local Islamic center. In North Dakota, someone torched

Leaders of the Council on American-Islamic Relations held a press conference to condemn the San Bernardino shooting and to support the victims' families.

a Somali restaurant. The incidents were underscored by tweets from then presidential candidate Donald Trump, who called for a complete ban on all Muslims entering the United States.

In a speech on December 6, 2015, President Obama called the San Bernardino attack an act of terror. "It is clear that the two of them had gone down the dark path of radicalization, embracing a perverted interpretation of Islam that calls for war against America and the West," he said, going on to outline the United States' ongoing fight against ISIS.[8] Obama spent a portion of his speech focusing on the need for the nation to stay united and not identify all Muslims with extremists. "We cannot turn against one another by letting this fight be defined as a war between America and Islam," he said. "That, too, is what groups like [ISIS] want."[9]

CONTRASTING HEADLINES

A 2018 study by the University of Alabama found that terrorist attacks committed by Islamic extremists between 2006 and 2015 received 357 percent more press coverage in the United States than attacks committed by non-Muslims. Researchers found that attacks committed by non-Muslims got an average of 15 headlines, but attacks by Islamic extremists got 105 headlines. In reality, right-wing extremists committed nearly twice as many terror attacks in that time frame.[10]

CHAPTER SEVEN

DEEP
DIVIDES

On June 12, 2016, approximately 300 people were gathered at Pulse, an LGBTQ nightclub in Orlando, Florida.[1] The club was known as a welcoming, safe place for those in the LGBTQ community and other patrons of many ages and backgrounds. That night, the busy venue became the scene of a devastating attack. At about 2:00 a.m., 29-year-old Omar Mateen, carrying a semiautomatic rifle and semiautomatic pistol, began shooting inside. People ran for the exits or fell to the floor after being hit, while others crawled to safety or tried to hide in other parts of the building. An off-duty police officer working as a security guard exchanged gunfire with Mateen before calling for backup. People trapped

Police set up an extensive presence outside the Pulse nightclub in the aftermath of the shooting there.

MOTIVES IN ORLANDO

As they uncovered more information about the Orlando shooter's life, intelligence officials called his motives into question. According to journalist Dina Temple-Raston, authorities were soon "becoming increasingly convinced that the motive for this attack had very little—or maybe nothing—to do with ISIS."[3] Many people viewed the Orlando shooting as an intentional attack on the LGBTQ community. The FBI reported that it was investigating the role of antigay attitudes in the attack, and journalists noted that ISIS had often called for the murders of gay people. This targeting of the gay community could have also stemmed from Mateen's personal background. Analysts pointed out that people who are self-radicalized over the internet often do not follow a straightforward set of beliefs and can even contradict the groups they claim to be following. The true motives of the Orlando shooter will never be known for certain.

inside called or texted loved ones and tried to call 911. "He's gonna kill us," one man quietly told a 911 dispatcher from his hiding place.[2]

The shooter told police he pledged allegiance to ISIS. The rampage turned into a hostage situation as the gunman refused to surrender. Authorities tried to negotiate with him while assessing the validity of his threats about explosives he claimed to have hidden in the building. They also tried to rescue people from other parts of the building. Eight people were rescued when officers removed an air conditioning unit from the wall.

The three-hour standoff ended when officers rushed the building, driving an armored vehicle through a wall and tossing in stun grenades. The gunman shot more hostages before being killed in the ensuing shoot-out. In all, 49 people were killed and another 53 were wounded.[4] The attack at Pulse was the deadliest mass shooting in US history until it was surpassed by a massacre in Las Vegas, Nevada, the next year. On October 1, 2017, from the 32nd floor of a Las Vegas Strip hotel, gunman Stephen Paddock shot into a crowd, killing 58 people and injuring hundreds of others before killing himself.

Shortly after the Orlando shooting, President Obama said the attack was the result of homegrown extremism. "We know enough to say this was an act of terror and act of hate," he said.[5] Mateen was born in New York. Many groups were quick to label the attack as a hate crime or domestic terrorism. "This is a hate crime, plain and simple," said CAIR's national communications director, Ibrahim Hooper. "We condemn it in the strongest possible terms."[6]

President Obama, *left*, and Vice President Joe Biden visit a memorial for the victims of the Pulse nightclub shooting.

SELF-RADICALIZED TERRORISTS

Questions quickly arose regarding Mateen's motivations and weapons. He had legally purchased his guns in Florida, although he had been placed on—and later removed from—an FBI terrorist watch list a few years prior. "An evil person came in here and legally purchased two firearms from us," said the gun store owner, Ed Henson. "I'm sorry he picked my place. I wish he'd picked nowhere."[7] After the Pulse shooting, familiar debates swirled, with many lawmakers calling for gun safety reforms and background checks. Others backed by the National Rifle Association (NRA) called gun laws an infringement on the Second Amendment to the US Constitution. The type of semiautomatic rifle Mateen used had been outlawed in 1994 under President Bill Clinton as part of a federal

GUN DEBATE

After a federal ban on semiautomatic weapons expired in 2004, AR-15-style weapons were used for several well-known mass shootings, including the 2012 Sandy Hook elementary school shooting in Connecticut that killed 27 children and adults. Analysts reported that if the ban had still been in place, Mateen may not have been able to legally purchase his gun or similar semiautomatic firearms, but they couldn't be sure without knowing all the add-ons Mateen's weapon had. In 2013, Senator Dianne Feinstein of California had proposed a bill for a federal ban on assault weapons that would have outlawed similar firearms, but it was voted down in the Senate.

weapons ban. The ban had been allowed to expire in 2004 under President George W. Bush's administration.

In the days after the Orlando attack, Florida gun sales increased significantly. The Florida Department of Law Enforcement reported that background checks for gun purchases more than doubled from the same time frame the year before. Meanwhile, the US Senate rejected four measures

"ANYONE WITH A COMPUTER CAN SELF-RADICALIZE. IF YOU LOOK LONG ENOUGH ONLINE, YOU CAN FIND JUSTIFICATION FOR ANYTHING, BUT THAT DOESN'T MAKE IT RIGHT OR TRUE."[8]

—FBI SPECIAL AGENT, 2018

meant to expand background checks and block the sale of guns to people on terrorist watch lists. Two measures had been introduced by Democrats, while the other two were put forth by Republicans. The proposals differed in details that neither side would compromise on, and as a result, none of the measures passed.

Mateen appeared to have been radicalized online, inspired at least partly by extremist information on the internet. Mateen reportedly had checked Facebook during the shooting to see if the news was trending. Like many other self-radicalized terrorists, Mateen did not seem to have had direct contact with terror groups such as

ISIS. As in San Bernardino, the radicalization of Mateen illustrated a growing threat. Using social media, terrorists of all ideologies could influence others to commit violence.

HATE IN CHARLOTTESVILLE

On the night of August 11, 2017, neo-Nazis, KKK members, white nationalists, and other far-right supporters marched through the University of Virginia campus in Charlottesville. Some held weapons, flags with hate group symbols, or signs with racist and anti-Semitic phrases. They chanted white supremacy slogans such as "Jews will not replace us" and "white lives matter."[9]

They were part of the Unite the Right rally, organized by white nationalist leaders. Although the event was supposedly held to protest the Charlottesville City Council's vote to remove Confederate statues from public spaces, organizers hoped to rally support for white supremacy and the alt-right movement—a largely online-based group of people who believed the white race was under threat. "If you want to defend the South and Western civilization from the Jew and his dark-skinned allies, be at Charlottesville on 12 August," one organizer

White supremacists were met by anti-racist counterprotesters during the Unite the Right rally in Charlottesville.

tweeted.[10] The event attracted people from across the country. In addition to the white supremacists, there were many counterprotesters, including some far-left supporters calling themselves anti-fascists, who showed up to rally against them.

The following day, Virginia's governor declared a state of emergency, and police declared the rally an unlawful gathering. The white supremacists, many dressed in riot gear, clashed with the counterprotesters. Tensions came to a head that afternoon when 20-year-old James Alex Fields Jr. from Ohio intentionally plowed his car into a crowd of counterprotesters before speeding away. This killed counterprotester Heather Heyer, age 32, and injured 19 others.[11] Fields had been seen earlier marching with a Nazi hate group. As the nation reeled from the violence, a familiar debate was heating up.

CHAPTER EIGHT

QUESTIONS OF
TERRORISM

Following the violence at the Unite the Right rally in Charlottesville, many leaders, including Charlottesville mayor Michael Signer, US national security adviser H. R. McMaster, and US attorney general Jeff Sessions, condemned Heather Heyer's death as an act of domestic terrorism. Citizens and lawmakers called for Fields to be charged as a domestic terrorist. However, as had happened many times in recent years after shocking acts of violence, experts weighed in to explain that, although the government had a definition of domestic terrorism, it did not have a federal criminal charge of domestic terrorism.

The Charlottesville case sparked new debates around the topic. Some said it was time to make

As people mourned the loss of counterprotester Heather Heyer, many officials labeled her murder as domestic terrorism.

domestic terrorism a federal crime. CNN legal analyst Page Pate, a criminal defense and constitutional lawyer, said that rather than try to prosecute such cases as federal hate crimes or other crimes, a specific domestic terrorism law should be put in place. "It would send a much more powerful message to groups that support and promote this kind of violence to call it what it is and allow for federal prosecution of these crimes as terrorism," Pate said.[1]

Others disagreed, saying a new law would complicate the situation more than it would help. Groups such as the ACLU said a federal domestic terrorism charge was unneeded and would risk criminalizing someone's beliefs rather than their actions. They warned that such a law could be used by one political group against another. Still others argued that a sufficient amount of state

CROSSING THE LINE

The violence at Charlottesville highlighted the continuing challenge counterterrorism officials faced in reconciling extremism and free speech. Speaking out with racist beliefs was not a crime. However, once those beliefs crossed into violence or advocating violence or crime, authorities could step in. Some people involved in the Unite the Right rally were charged with conspiracy to riot. When US attorney for the Western District of Virginia Thomas T. Cullen announced sentencing against three members of a California-based white supremacy group, he said, "These avowed white supremacists traveled to Charlottesville to incite and commit acts of violence, not to engage in peaceful First Amendment expression."[2]

and federal laws already existed to prosecute extremists with other crimes, such as murder, tax violations, crimes related to threats, or crimes related to illegal firearms. On the news website Politico, terrorism experts Brian Michael Jenkins and Richard C. Daddario asked, "Should anger about taxes, believing abortion is a sin, or excessive zeal in protecting the environment arouse suspicion?"[3] They wrote that trying to create a domestic terrorism law would be challenging and ultimately unhelpful.

> "THE WHITE NATIONALIST RALLY IN CHARLOTTESVILLE, VIRGINIA, WAS A WAKE-UP CALL ABOUT HOW RACIAL HATRED WAS MOVING INTO ORGANIZED VIOLENCE."[4]
>
> —HANNAH ALLAM, *NPR*, 2019

Amid this renewed debate, the law remained unchanged. Meanwhile, Fields was convicted in state court on charges including first-degree murder, malicious wounding, and leaving the scene of an accident. He pleaded guilty to 29 federal hate crime charges. He was sentenced to life in prison.

THE NEW ANARCHISTS

The events in Charlottesville thrust another group into the spotlight: an anarchist movement looking to counter the right-wing extremism and racism of white supremacists. Loosely connected anti-fascist groups known as antifa had grown since Donald Trump's successful presidential campaign in 2016. The movement was difficult for authorities to fully understand, as some people who identified as antifa were anti-racist or socialist groups, clergy, or others who practiced nonviolence. The movement itself, however, was widely understood to be made up of violent extremists. "It was in that period [as the Trump campaign emerged] that we really became aware of them," a senior law enforcement official said. "These Antifa guys were showing up with weapons, shields, and bike helmets and just beating [people]. . . . They're starting fires; they're throwing bombs and smashing windows."[5]

Antifa members, who represented a small portion of the counterprotesters in Charlottesville, soon became symbols of the violent response to white supremacists as the clashes between the two groups intensified. In 2017, the FBI and the Department of Homeland Security classified antifa's activities as domestic terrorism and placed some of their members on US terrorism watch lists.

A member of the far-right group Proud Boys, which is also known for violent extremism, holds up a sign protesting the far-left antifa.

However, officials said they still did not fully understand the motivation and connections of the antifa groups.

STATUS OF TERROR

From 2017 to 2019, right-wing extremists stayed in the news for committing the majority of domestic terrorism attacks. According to analysis by the online magazine *Quartz*, using data from University of Maryland's Global Terrorism Database, two-thirds of domestic terrorism attacks in 2018 were right-wing extremism. The magazine explained that these attacks had "racist, anti-Muslim, homophobic, anti-Semitic, fascist, anti-government, or xenophobic motivations."[6]

In a 2019 congressional hearing, FBI officials said the number of domestic terrorism attacks had increased over the past two years, with arrests and deaths caused by domestic terrorists outnumbering those by international terrorists. According to Michael McGarrity, assistant director of the FBI's counterterrorism division, approximately 50 percent of the FBI's 850 open domestic terrorism cases were "antigovernment, antiauthority," while 40 percent were "racially motivated violent extremism cases," the majority of which were of white supremacists.[7] Although the FBI said domestic terrorism was a priority, the agency was still using more resources on international terrorism cases. Eighty percent of its counterterrorism cases involved international terrorism. Those cases included homegrown extremists inspired by ISIS or similar groups. The remaining 20 percent were domestic terrorism cases.[8]

A MATTER OF WORDS

Government leaders and presidential administrations have received criticism for their response to white supremacists and extremism. The issue escalated under President Trump, who had made inflammatory remarks regarding immigrants, congresswomen of color, Mexicans, Muslims, and others. The president received vocal support from right-wing extremist groups, but his supporters argued that he had no control over those who supported him. Critics of Trump said political leaders should be more persistent in disavowing racist and white supremacist groups. They said that a lack of public disapproval from political leaders legitimized and encouraged extremists' views.

TO CATCH A TERRORIST

Counterterrorism officials often turn to the public for help in preventing terrorist attacks. According to the FBI website, approximately one in four internationally inspired domestic terrorism attacks in recent years has been disrupted using tips from community leaders and the public. Together with the National Counterterrorism Center and the Department of Homeland Security, the FBI has created a public booklet to assist in identifying behaviors that could be associated with terrorism. First published in 2017, "Homegrown Violent Extremist Mobilization Indicators" describes behaviors and whether they might be constitutionally protected activities or should be reported to law enforcement. "We can't be everywhere," McGarrity said in 2019. "We count on our partners to identify threats in their communities."[10]

In August 2019, Trump used strong language to condemn violence following the El Paso and Dayton shootings. "In one voice, our nation must condemn racism, bigotry, and white supremacy," he said. "These sinister ideologies must be defeated. Hate has no place in America."[11]

This debate highlighted concerns that authorities were not adequately addressing the problem of right-wing extremism under Trump's administration. FBI director Christopher Wray said the agency treated extremist groups as a priority. However, according to former FBI supervisor Dave Gomez, writing in the *Washington Post*, "There's some reluctance among agents to bring forth an investigation that targets what the president perceives as his base."

President Trump speaks with reporters while visiting El Paso shortly after the 2019 Walmart shooting there.

He called it a "no-win situation."[12] Some conservative media personalities seemed reluctant to acknowledge the problem of right-wing extremism, with Fox News host Tucker Carlson calling white supremacy a "hoax" in 2019.[13]

Meanwhile, the FBI warned that online conspiracy theories were an emerging domestic terrorism threat. The theories often spread quickly online and could inspire people with violent agendas. As just one example, the FBI pointed to Pizzagate, a 2016 conspiracy theory spread on social media, online forums, and far-right media sites. It claimed that top Democratic politicians were part of a child abuse ring based out of a pizza restaurant in Washington, DC. The story resulted in a North Carolina man going to the pizzeria to investigate and firing his rifle inside. Viral online conspiracy theories would continue.

REPORTING ON CONSPIRACY THEORIES

Media faces a challenge when reporting on conspiracy theories so as not to bring more attention to extremist causes. For instance, the El Paso gunman's manifesto referenced a conspiracy theory popular among white nationalists, known as the "great replacement," which theorized that nonwhite people would replace white people. According to Rosa Schwartzburg of the *Guardian* newspaper, "It is vital that we understand the origins and implications of the theory, even as we strive to diminish its platform."[14]

CHAPTER NINE

SEARCHING FOR
A SOLUTION

Following a number of attacks in 2019, including a synagogue shooting in Philadelphia and the shooting at the El Paso Walmart, lawmakers and citizens renewed calls for a federal domestic terrorism law. In 2019, California Democratic representative Adam Schiff and Arizona Republican senator Martha McSally introduced similar bills that would give the government the power to prosecute crimes as domestic terrorism. The bills would also make it a crime to offer support to terrorists by providing money, transportation, or training. "The bill I am introducing will give federal law enforcement the tools they have asked for so that they can punish criminals to the fullest extent of the law," McSally said.[1]

People continued to point to white supremacy as a source of domestic terrorism throughout 2019.

Proponents of the bills said a domestic terrorism law would help the FBI in preventing an attack before it happened. They said having a formal charge of domestic terrorism would show that the government takes white supremacy as seriously as other types of terrorism. Critics, as in past arguments, held that a new law would create more problems, such as encouraging government overreach and spurring groups to use the laws against freedom of speech. They said the law would not help curb terrorism or assist in bringing charges against attackers.

Republicans and Democrats alike also called for discussion around gun laws. Possible changes included expanding background checks required before purchasing a gun and creating "red flag" laws, which would give authorities power to take away weapons from those deemed dangerous. Another proposed change was to limit

TERRORISM PREVENTED

In February 2019, an act of domestic terrorism was prevented with the arrest of an active duty Coast Guard lieutenant. Authorities in Maryland arrested 49-year-old Christopher Paul Hasson, who called himself a white nationalist. Hasson had been stockpiling weapons for years and planned to stage attacks against top Democrats, TV personalities, and activists. Court documents described him as a domestic terrorist who plotted to "murder innocent civilians on a scale rarely seen in this country."[2] He was charged with illegal weapons and drug charges and was sentenced to more than 13 years in prison.

the straw purchases of guns, situations in which someone legitimately buys a gun for someone who is not allowed to make the purchase.

BREAKING UP THE BASE

In January 2020, authorities arrested members of a white supremacist neo-Nazi group called The Base in separate incidents. The group was founded in 2018 with the purpose of overthrowing the government, starting a race war, and establishing a white-only nation, according to law enforcement. The FBI reported the group organized military-style training camps. Members also used encrypted online chat rooms and devices to discuss violence against Black Americans, Jewish Americans, and other groups. Members of The Base also used social media to promote their agenda.

In Maryland, the FBI arrested three men on charges including illegal transport of a machine gun. One of the men was Canadian and had entered the United States

"WE HAVE NOT SEEN THE INTENSITY AND FOCUS ON WHERE THE PROBLEM REALLY IS—RIGHT-WING RADICAL TERRORISM."[3]

—REPRESENTATIVE BENNIE THOMPSON, CHAIR OF THE HOUSE HOMELAND SECURITY COMMITTEE, 2019

illegally. Two of the men had military training. The group had planned to attend a progun rally in Richmond, Virginia. According to authorities, the group had illegally helped the Canadian member cross the northern US border and had worked to build an illegal semiautomatic rifle.

In Georgia, police arrested three other members of The Base who were allegedly plotting to kill members of antifa. An undercover FBI agent was able to infiltrate the group online before being welcomed as a member. According to court documents, the group made the undercover

An arrested member of the violent white supremacist group The Base speaks with his lawyers in court in February 2020.

agent perform military-type drills to prepare for what they called "the boogaloo," a term for a theoretical second Civil War. Separately, another member of The Base accused of vandalizing a synagogue in Wisconsin was charged with conspiracy. The vandalism was reportedly part of a larger series of attacks on minority-owned property throughout the country.

LOOKING AHEAD

In February 2020, FBI director Christopher Wray reported to the House Judiciary Committee that more deaths had been caused by domestic terrorists than international terrorists in recent years. The FBI considered the top domestic terrorism threat to be that from racially motivated violent extremists, called RMVEs, who had carried out most of the deadly attacks in 2018 and 2019. Without specifying groups, Wray said those attackers have been the most lethal of all domestic terrorism movements since 2001. He also reported that the FBI was most concerned about lone offender attacks, with shootings being the most common mode of attack. He shared that in 2019, the FBI had created the Domestic Terrorism-Hate

Crimes Fusion Cell, a group of experts from the Criminal Investigative Division and the Counterterrorism Division to help investigate current threats and prevent future attacks. According to Wray, the FBI had more than 1,000 violent extremist cases in progress throughout all 50 states.[4]

While white supremacist attacks made up the majority of recent domestic terror attacks, doubts remained among some that political leaders or federal agencies were taking the problem as seriously as they did for jihadist extremism. The SPLC reported that its number of identified white nationalist groups rose for the second straight year in 2019, a 55 percent increase since 2017.[5] It also warned of a significant increase in anti-LGBTQ hate groups. Federal law enforcement and national security officials have reported warnings of far-right extremism being ignored over the past decade. Some officials have said it may be too late to stop the momentum of white supremacist groups. "I'm afraid we've reached a tipping point where we're in for this kind of violence for a long time," Daryl Johnson, a former senior analyst at the Department of Homeland Security, said in 2019.[7]

One of the biggest challenges for agencies countering terrorism is likely to be technology. Cyber threats have continued to develop in size and sophistication, making them more difficult to investigate. The internet and social media increasingly blur the lines between domestic and international terror movements. "Terrorism today— including domestic terrorism—moves at the speed of social media," Wray said in 2020.[8] The FBI reported that it was closely monitoring an emerging trend of extremists such as neo-Nazis communicating with like-minded foreign extremists. The FBI was also working with partners in other countries to investigate people who could be radicalizing the United States' domestic terrorists.

MORE TO THE
STORY

COMBATING THE
INCEL MOVEMENT

In the late 2010s, law enforcement warned of the dangers of a rising movement of misogynistic men connected to a number of violent attacks. The men, who call themselves incels, advocate violence against both women and men who they see as being successful in relationships. The term *incel* comes from the phrase "involuntary celibate," referring to these men's anger at wanting a sexual partner but not having one. Like other contemporary extremist groups, they have found support, motivation, and growing attention online. According to a study by the Texas Department of Public Safety, published in 2020, men associated with the incel movement were an emerging domestic terrorist threat. However, as with many violent domestic groups, there is debate over whether incel attackers should be considered terrorists. The incel movement has made headlines with much-publicized national and global attacks committed by men holding this viewpoint. Attacks by self-identified incels included a 2014 shooting at a University of California-Santa Barbara sorority house and a 2019 shooting at a Florida yoga studio. One of the challenges authorities have encountered while trying to combat the incel movement, as with many extremist groups, is the movement's lack of a clear organization. Violence is often carried out by lone attackers. The movement has since had overlaps with those of far-right terrorists, with those who embrace white supremacy finding common ground in the idea of male supremacy.

UNITY AMID VIOLENCE

Domestic terrorism has been a part of the United States since its beginning. The extremist groups willing to carry out attacks have shifted over the years. Some have burst onto the scene and been dismantled quickly, while others have lingered for decades. Groups have included white supremacists, religious extremists, environmental extremists, national or cultural separatists, and others with radical views. Motivated by a wide variety of extremist causes, lone attackers have created mass destruction and terror, murdering and maiming innocent people. The toll of these attacks will last forever in the minds of survivors, victims' loved ones, first responders, and medical staff.

MEDICAL RESPONSE

In addition to law enforcement, hospitals must respond quickly in the event of a domestic terrorism attack. When scores of injured people are brought to hospitals, workers must leap into action to treat the most seriously wounded, quickly clean up the blood between patients, and scramble to refill their blood supplies. The traumatic injuries caused by semiautomatic weapons are particularly serious. Following the Orlando shooting, a hospital trauma director described the situation as a "war scene."[9]

Law enforcement has continued working to stay one step ahead to prevent attacks before they happen, with varying results. As technology has evolved, so has its use by terrorist groups and radicalized individuals. Authorities have continued looking to technology to help prevent and track terrorist attacks. While extremists utilize social media and technology to communicate, recruit, and promote their agendas, authorities can also use technology to help capture domestic terrorists and bring charges against them.

Community members often gather to support each other in the wake of domestic terrorism attacks, including after the El Paso Walmart shooting.

As families and communities mourn some lives taken and others forever changed, citizens and lawmakers have continued to discuss the best ways to address extremism and how it relates to free speech, gun laws, politics, racism, religion, misogyny, and homophobia. After a domestic terror attack, people often ask whether a federal domestic terrorism law would be beneficial. In 2020, the opposing sides had not come to an agreement on whether to pass such a law.

Through the years, the nation has continued to show resilience in the face of terror and tragedy. Often individuals and groups that have been targets of attacks have responded with unity as their communities have rallied behind them. They have held prayer services and vigils, donated blood and necessary supplies, hung supportive posters and flags in their windows, advocated for legislative reform, started dialogues with other groups, and shown other signs of solidarity, vowing to be stronger than ever.

ESSENTIAL
FACTS

MAJOR EVENTS

- From 1978 to 1996, the FBI carries out a manhunt for Ted Kaczynski, known as the Unabomber, who was responsible for a series of bombings that killed three people and injured 23 others.

- On September 11, 2001, the United States experiences an attack by the foreign terrorist group al-Qaeda. The attack kills nearly 3,000 people and changes national conversations about terrorism.

- In 2015, white supremacist Dylann Roof kills nine Black people at a church in Charleston, South Carolina. The attack highlights acts of violence committed by white supremacists.

- In 2016, jihadist extremist attacker Omar Mateen kills 49 and injures 53 in an attack on the gay nightclub Pulse in Orlando, Florida.

- In 2019, Patrick Crusius kills 23 people and injures more than 20 others at a Walmart in El Paso, Texas, in a racist attack against Hispanic people.

KEY PLAYERS

- US president George W. Bush signed the 2001 USA PATRIOT Act into law following the September 11, 2001, terrorist attacks.

- US president Donald Trump became known for divisive language around issues of race. His election saw the rise of antifa groups.

- Southern Poverty Law Center is an organization that monitors and tracks hate groups and extremist activities.

IMPACT ON SOCIETY

Most deadly terror attacks in the United States are carried out by domestic terrorists. Through the decades, homegrown extremist groups and lone attackers have included white supremacists, religious extremists, environmental extremists, cultural separatists, and others with radical views. Law enforcement has faced new challenges with the internet allowing extremists to be radicalized online and communicate to wide audiences. Citizens and lawmakers have continued to discuss the best ways to address domestic terrorism. Many states have some form of anti-terrorism laws, but there is no law that makes domestic terrorism a federal crime.

QUOTE

"We know enough to say this was an act of terror and act of hate."

—President Barack Obama, on the Pulse nightclub shooting

GLOSSARY

ANARCHIST
A person who believes countries should not have governments.

CAPITALIST
Having to do with an economic system in which businesses are privately owned and operated for the purpose of making a profit.

CIVILIAN
A person who is not a member of the police or military.

COMMUNISM
A political system in which the government controls the economy and owns all property.

CONSPIRACY THEORY
A belief, without proof, that someone is responsible for an event or crime.

COURT-MARTIAL
A trial for members of the military in a special court because they are accused of breaking military law.

EXTREMIST

A person who has extreme or fanatical political or religious views and often advocates violence.

FASCIST

A person who believes in a government structure in which a powerful leader puts national considerations ahead of the freedoms of individual citizens and opposition is suppressed.

MISOGYNISTIC

Having hatred of or contempt for women.

PROPAGANDA

Information that carries facts or details slanted to favor a single point of view or political bias.

RADICAL

Supporting political reform by changing social structures and values.

SEGREGATED

Separated based on race, gender, ethnicity, or other factors.

SUPREMACIST

Someone who believes people of a particular race, religion, or other category are better than other people.

XENOPHOBIC

Exhibiting a dislike, distrust, or fear of people from other countries.

ADDITIONAL
RESOURCES

SELECTED BIBLIOGRAPHY

Allam, Hannah. "2019 Marks a Turning Point in How the U.S. Confronts Domestic Terrorism." *NPR*, 26 Dec. 2019, npr.org. Accessed 28 Mar. 2020.

Jenkins, Brian Michael, and Richard C. Daddario. "Think Mass Shootings Are Terrorism? Careful What You Wish For." *Politico*, 7 Nov. 2017, politico.com. Accessed 7 Mar. 2020.

Wilber, Del Quentin. "FBI Struggles to Confront Right-Wing Terrorism." *Los Angeles Times*, 11 Aug. 2019, latimes.com. Accessed 27 Mar. 2020.

FURTHER READINGS

Harris, Duchess, and Jennifer Simms. *Mass Shootings in America*. Abdo, 2019.

Kennon, Caroline. *Battling Terrorism*. Lucent, 2018.

Wiener, Gary, ed. *Domestic Terrorism*. Greenhaven, 2020.

ONLINE RESOURCES

To learn more about domestic terrorism,
please visit **abdobooklinks.com** or scan this
QR code. These links are routinely monitored
and updated to provide the most current
information available.

MORE INFORMATION

For more information on this subject, contact or visit the
following organizations:

Federal Bureau of Investigation Headquarters
935 Pennsylvania Ave. NW
Washington, DC 20535
202-324-3000
fbi.gov
The FBI is a federal law enforcement agency that investigates
domestic terrorism.

Southern Poverty Law Center
400 Washington Ave.
Montgomery, AL 36104
334-956-8200
splcenter.org
The Southern Poverty Law Center advocates for civil rights and tracks
and monitors hate groups.

SOURCE
NOTES

CHAPTER 1. TERROR IN EL PASO

1. "Walmart Will Reopen El Paso Store Where Gunman Killed 22 People." *NBC News*, 22 Aug. 2019, nbcnews.com. Accessed 28 Mar. 2020.

2. Vic Kolenc. "Walmart Manager Says El Paso Shooting Won't Change 'My Passion for My People' or Community." *El Paso Times*, 8 Aug. 2019, elpasotimes.com. Accessed 28 Mar. 2020.

3. Chas Danner. "Everything We Know about the El Paso Walmart Massacre." *Intelligencer*, 7 Aug. 2019, nymag.com. Accessed 11 Aug. 2020.

4. Danner, "Everything We Know about the El Paso Walmart Massacre."

5. Vera Bergengruen and W. J. Hennigan. "'We Are Being Eaten from Within.' Why America Is Losing the Battle against White Nationalist Terrorism.'" *Time*, 8 Aug. 2019, time.com. Accessed 22 Apr. 2020.

6. "El Paso Walmart Shooting Victim Dies, Raising Death Toll to 23." *NBC News*, 26 Apr. 2020, nbcnews.com. Accessed 11 Aug. 2020.

7. Adeel Hassan. "Dayton Gunman Shot 26 People in 32 Seconds, Police Timeline Reveals." *New York Times*, 13 Aug. 2019, nytimes.com. Accessed 11 Aug. 2020.

8. Lisa Daniels. "Prosecuting Terrorism in State Court." *Lawfare*, 26 Oct. 2016, lawfareblog.com. Accessed 28 Mar. 2020.

9. Karma Allen. "Why Domestic Terror Designation in El Paso Shootings Likely Won't Result in Terrorism Charges." *ABC News*, 6 Aug. 2019, abcnews.go.com. Accessed 28 Mar. 2020.

10. Nathaniel Meyersohn. "Walmart Ends All Handgun Ammunition Sales and Asks Customers Not to Carry Guns into Stores." *CNN*, 3 Sept. 2019, cnn.com. Accessed 23 Apr. 2020.

11. Allen, "Domestic Terror Designation in El Paso."

12. Cedar Attanasio. "Man Charged in Walmart Shooting Appears in Federal Court." *AP News*, 12 Feb. 2020, apnews.com. Accessed 29 Mar. 2020.

13. Bergengruen and Hennigan, "'We Are Being Eaten from Within.'"

14. "Why Do People Become Violent Extremists?" *FBI*, n.d., fbi.gov. Accessed 22 Apr. 2020.

15. Margot Williams and Trevor Aaronson. "How Individual States Have Criminalized Terrorism." *Intercept*, 23 Mar. 2019, theintercept.com. Accessed 11 Aug. 2020.

CHAPTER 2. EARLY FORMS OF TERROR

1. Kurtis Lee. "Q&A: 'Capital Punishment Is the Stepchild of Lynching.' Here's What Bryan Stevenson Hopes to Address with a Memorial Honoring Black People Who Were Killed." *Los Angeles Times*, 26 Apr. 2018, latimes.com. Accessed 9 Apr. 2020.

2. Richard Maxwell Brown. *Strain of Violence: Historical Studies of American Violence and Vigilantism.* Oxford UP, 1977. 21.

3. Lee, "Q&A: 'Capital Punishment.'"

4. "Ku Klux Klan." *SPLC*, n.d., splcenter.org. Accessed 25 Apr. 2020.

5. "The Early Labor Movement." *History Detectives*, 2014, pbs.org. Accessed 10 Apr. 2020.

6. "The 1910 Bombing of the Los Angeles Times Has Been the Subject of Books and Film. Now It's a Bus Tour." *Los Angeles Times*, 22 Sept. 2017, latimes.com. Accessed 11 Aug. 2020.

7. Evan Andrews. "The Mysterious Wall Street Bombing, 95 Years Ago." *History*, 7 Mar. 2019, history.com. Accessed 23 Apr. 2020.

8. Andrews, "The Mysterious Wall Street Bombing."

9. Kelly Wallace. "Forgotten Los Angeles History: The Chinese Massacre of 1871." *Los Angeles Public Library*, 19 May 2017, lapl.org. Accessed 12 Apr. 2020.

10. "1921 Tulsa Race Massacre." *Tulsa Historical Society and Museum*, 2020, tulsahistory.org. Accessed 10 Apr. 2020.

CHAPTER 3. THE 1960s AND 1970s

1. Bryan Burrough. "The Bombings of America that We Forgot." *Time*, 20 Sept. 2016, time.com. Accessed 11 Apr. 2020.

2. Peter Bergen and Courtney Schuster. "The Golden Age of Terrorism." *CNN*, 21 Aug. 2015, cnn.com. Accessed 11 Apr. 2020.

3. Roberta Belli. "Effects and Effectiveness of Law Enforcement Intelligence Measures to Counter Homegrown Terrorism: A Case Study on the Fuerzas Armadas De Liberación Nacional (FALN)." *US Department of Homeland Security*, 2012, start.umd.edu. Accessed 11 Apr. 2020.

4. "Weather Underground Bombings." *FBI*, n.d., fbi.gov. Accessed 11 Apr. 2020.

5. Lila Thulin. "In the 1980s, a Far-Left, Female-Led Domestic Terrorism Group Bombed the U.S. Capitol." *Smithsonian Magazine*, 6 Jan. 2020, smithsonianmag.com. Accessed 11 Apr. 2020.

6. "The Weather Underground: The Movement." *PBS: Independent Lens*, n.d., pbs.org. Accessed 12 Aug. 2020.

7. "LAPD Raid Leaves Six SLA Members Dead." *History*, 14 May 2020, history.com. Accessed 11 Aug. 2020.

8. "Patty Hearst." *FBI*, n.d., fbi.gov. Accessed 11 Apr. 2020.

CHAPTER 4. EMERGENCE OF THE LONE ATTACKER

1. William Finnegan. "When the Unabomber Was Arrested, One of the Longest Manhunts in FBI History Was Finally Over." *Smithsonian Magazine*, May 2018, smithsonianmag.com. Accessed 18 Apr. 2020.

2. Muriel Pearson, Spencer Wilking, and Lauren Effron. "Survivors of 1993 Waco Siege Describe What Happened in Fire that Ended the 51-Day Standoff." *ABC News*, 3 Jan. 2018, abcnews.go.com. Accessed 17 Apr. 2020.

3. Pearson, Wilking, and Effron. "Survivors of 1993 Waco Siege."

4. Meghan Keneally. "Ruby Ridge Siege, 25 Years Later, a 'Rallying Cry' for Today's White Nationalists." *ABC News*, 18 Aug. 2017, abcnews.go.com. Accessed 11 Apr. 2020.

5. "Oklahoma City Bombing." *FBI*, n.d., fbi.gov. Accessed 11 Aug. 2020.

6. Dan Herbeck and Lou Michel. "PrimeTime: McVeigh's Own Words." *ABC News*, 6 Jan. 2006, abcnews.go.com. Accessed 11 Aug. 2020.

7. Robert Jimison. "How the FBI Smashed White Supremacist Group The Order." *CNN*, 21 Aug. 2018, cnn.com. Accessed 19 Apr. 2020.

8. Finnegan, "When the Unabomber Was Arrested."

9. Dave Davies. "FBI Profiler Says Linguistic Work Was Pivotal in Capture of Unabomber." *NPR*, 22 Aug. 2017, npr.org. Accessed 19 Apr. 2020.

CHAPTER 5. A TURNING POINT

1. J. T. Caruso. "Before the House Subcommittee on National Security, Veterans Affairs, and International Relations." *FBI*, 21 Mar. 2002, archives.fbi.gov. Accessed 19 Apr. 2020.

2. "Anthrax: The Threat." *US CDC*, 1 Aug. 2014, cdc.gov. Accessed 19 Apr. 2020.

3. Brian Michael Jenkins. "The 1970s and the Birth of Contemporary Terrorism." *Hill*, 30 July 2015, thehill.com. Accessed 10 Apr. 2020.

4. Terry Frieden. "FBI, ATF Address Domestic Terrorism." *CNN*, 19 May 2005, cnn.com. Accessed 19 Apr. 2020.

5. "ACLU Statement on the Violent Radicalization and Homegrown Terrorism Prevention Act of 2007." *American Civil Liberties Union*, 28 Nov. 2007, aclu.org. Accessed 24 Apr. 2020.

6. "Terrorism 2002/2005." *FBI*, n.d., fbi.gov. Accessed 18 Apr. 2020.

7. Alleen Brown. "The Green Scare." *Intercept*, 23 Mar. 2019, theintercept.com. Accessed 24 Apr. 2020.

SOURCE NOTES
CONTINUED

CHAPTER 6. EXTREMISM TAKES HOLD

1. "Army Major Kills 13 People in Fort Hood Shooting Spree." *History*, 4 Nov. 2019, history.com. Accessed 19 Apr. 2020.

2. Rick Jervis. "Witnesses at Hasan Trial Describe Carnage of Ft. Hood Shootings." *USA Today*, 8 Aug. 2013, usatoday.com. Accessed 19 Apr. 2020.

3. "Army Major Kills 13 People in Fort Hood Shooting Spree."

4. Lila Thulin. "In the 1980s, a Far-Left, Female-Led Domestic Terrorism Group Bombed the U.S. Capitol." *Smithsonian Magazine*, 6 Jan. 2020, smithsonianmag.com. Accessed 11 Apr. 2020.

5. "Durbin Chairs Hearing on Hate Crimes and the Threat of Domestic Extremism." *Dick Durbin Illinois*, 19 Sept. 2012, durbin.senate.gov. Accessed 23 Apr. 2020.

6. Rachel Kaadzi Ghansah. "A Most American Terrorist: The Making of Dylann Roof." *GQ*, 21 Aug. 2017, gq.com. Accessed 11 Aug. 2020.

7. "Heroism of San Bernardino Shooting Responders Lauded in Report." *Newsweek*, 10 Sept. 2016, newsweek.com. Accessed 11 Aug. 2020.

8. "President Obama Addresses the Nation on Keeping the American People Safe." *Medium*, 6 Dec. 2015, medium.com. Accessed 25 Apr. 2020.

9. "President Obama Addresses the Nation."

10. Mona Chalabi. "Terror Attacks by Muslims Receive 257% More Press Attention, Study Finds." *Guardian*, 20 July 2018, theguardian.com. Accessed 24 Apr. 2020.

CHAPTER 7. DEEP DIVIDES

1. Bart Jansen. "Weapons Gunman Used in Orlando Shooting Are High-Capacity, Common." *USA Today*, 15 June 2016, usatoday.com. Accessed 11 Aug. 2020.

2. Abigail Abrams. "911 Calls from Inside Pulse Orlando Nightclub Released: 'He's Gonna Kill Us.'" *Time*, 22 Sept. 2016, time.com. Accessed 20 Apr. 2020.

3. Merrit Kennedy. "Investigators Say Orlando Shooter Showed Few Warning Signs of Radicalization." *NPR*, 18 June 2016, npr.org. Accessed 26 Apr. 2020.

4. Ralph Ellis et al. "Orlando Shooting: 49 Killed, Shooter Pledged ISIS Allegiance." *CNN*, 13 June 2016, cnn.com. Accessed 20 Apr. 2020.

5. Ellis et al., "Orlando Shooting."

6. Ellis et al., "Orlando Shooting."

7. Matt Zapotosky and Mark Berman. "Orlando Gunman Who Pledged Loyalty to ISIS Was 'Homegrown' Extremist Radicalized Online, Obama Says." *Washington Post*, 13 June 2016, washingtonpost.com. Accessed 20 Apr. 2020.

8. "Terrorist Plot Foiled." *FBI*, 22 Oct. 2018, fbi.gov. Accessed 20 Apr. 2020.

9. Phil Helsel. "Two from White Supremacist Group Plead Guilty in Charlottesville Rally Violence." *NBC News*, 3 May 2019, nbcnews.com. Accessed 24 Apr. 2020.

10. Jane Coaston. "The Alt-Right Is Going on Trial in Charlottesville." *Vox*, 8 Mar. 2018, vox.com. Accessed 11 Aug. 2020.

11. Bill Morlin. "Study Shows Two-Thirds of U.S. Terrorism Tied to Right-Wing Extremists." *SPLC*, 12 Sept. 2018, splcenter.org. Accessed 23 Apr. 2020.

CHAPTER 8. QUESTIONS OF TERRORISM

1. Page Pate. "How Congress Has Dropped Ball on Domestic Terrorism." *CNN*, 14 Aug. 2017, cnn.com. Accessed 26 Apr. 2020.

2. Phil Helsel. "Two from White Supremacist Group Plead Guilty in Charlottesville Rally Violence." *NBC News*, 3 May 2019, nbcnews.com. Accessed 24 Apr. 2020.

3. Brian Michael Jenkins and Richard C. Daddario. "Think Mass Shootings Are Terrorism? Careful What You Wish For." *Politico*, 7 Nov. 2017, politico.com. Accessed 7 Mar. 2020.

4. Hannah Allam. "2019 Marks a Turning Point in How the U.S. Confronts Domestic Terrorism." *NPR*, 26 Dec. 2019, npr.org. Accessed 28 Mar. 2020.

5. Josh Meyer. "FBI, Homeland Security Warn of More 'Antifa' Attacks." *Politico*, 1 Sept. 2017, politico.com. Accessed 26 Apr. 2020.

6. Bill Morlin. "Study Shows Two-Thirds of U.S. Terrorism Tied to Right-Wing Extremists." *SPLC*, 12 Sept. 2018, splcenter.org. Accessed 23 Apr. 2020.

7. Mike Levine. "7 Key Questions about the Threat of Domestic Terrorism in America." *ABC News*, 6 Aug. 2019, abcnews.go.com. Accessed 23 Apr. 2020.

8. Levine, "7 Key Questions."

9. Adam Serwer. "The Terrorism that Doesn't Spark a Panic." *Atlantic*, 28 Jan. 2019, theatlantic.com. Accessed 24 Apr. 2020.

10. "The Homegrown Threat." *FBI*, 16 July 2019, fbi.gov. Accessed 24 Apr. 2020.

11. Domenico Montanaro. "Democratic Candidates Call Trump a White Supremacist, a Label Some Say Is 'Too Simple.'" *NPR*, 15 Aug. 2019, npr.org. Accessed 23 Apr. 2020.

12. Michelle Goldberg. "Opinion: Trump Is a White Nationalist Who Inspires Terrorism." *New York Times*, 5 Aug. 2019, nytimes.com. Accessed 23 Apr. 2020.

13. Bill McCarthy. "Fact-Checking Claims about the Mass Shootings in El Paso and Dayton." *Politifact*, 9 Aug. 2019, politifact.com. Accessed 27 Mar. 2020.

14. Rosa Schwartzburg. "The 'White Replacement Theory' Motivates Alt-Right Killers the World Over." *Guardian*, 5 Aug. 2019, theguardian.com. Accessed 24 Apr. 2020.

CHAPTER 9. SEARCHING FOR A SOLUTION

1. Burgess Everett. "GOP Sen. Martha McSally Drafts Bill Making Domestic Terrorism a Federal Crime." *Politico*, 14 Aug. 2019, politico.com. Accessed 24 Apr. 2020.

2. Greg Myre and Vanessa Romo. "Arrested Coast Guard Officer Allegedly Planned Attack 'on a Scale Rarely Seen.'" *NPR*, 20 Feb. 2019, npr.org. Accessed 11 Aug. 2020.

3. Del Quentin Wilber. "FBI Struggles to Confront Right-Wing Terrorism." *Los Angeles Times*, 11 Aug. 2019, latimes.com. Accessed 27 Mar. 2020.

4. Neil MacFarquhar. "As Domestic Terrorists Outpace Jihadists, New U.S. Law Is Debated." *New York Times*, 25 Feb. 2020, nytimes.com. Accessed 27 Mar. 2020.

5. "The Year in Hate and Extremism 2019." *SPLC*, 18 Mar. 2020, splcenter.org. Accessed 12 Apr. 2020.

6. "In Response to Booker Questioning, FBI Director Announces Agency No Longer Using Baseless 'Black Identity Extremists' Label." *Cory Booker*, 23 July 2019, booker.senate.gov. Accessed 26 Apr. 2020.

7. Vera Bergengruen and W. J. Hennigan. "'We Are Being Eaten from Within.'" *Time*, 8 Aug. 2019, time.com. Accessed 22 Apr. 2020.

8. Garrett M. Graff. "25 Years after Oklahoma City, Domestic Terrorism Is on the Rise." *Wired*, 19 Apr. 2020, wired.com. Accessed 24 Apr. 2020.

9. Rick Neale and John Bacon. "'This Is Not a Drill': Docs Detail Night in Orlando ER." *USA Today*, 15 June 2016, usatoday.com. Accessed 25 Apr. 2020.

INDEX

ABOUT THE
AUTHOR

LAURA K. MURRAY

Laura K. Murray is a Minnesota-based author of more than 80 books on subjects ranging from current events and pop culture to history and music.

ABOUT THE CONSULTANT

ORLANDREW E. DANZELL, PhD

Orlandrew E. Danzell, PhD, is currently an associate professor in the Intelligence Analysis Program, within the School of Integrated Sciences at James Madison University. Most recently, he was the chair of the Department of Intelligence Studies within the Ridge College at Mercyhurst University. His research focuses on conflict processes, transnational and domestic terrorism, military interventions, and intelligence theory and application.